Return to Me

a Blue Harbor novel

OLIVIA MILES

Rosewood Press

ALSO BY OLIVIA MILES

Blue Harbor Series
A Place for Us
Second Chance Summer
Because of You
Small Town Christmas

Stand-Alone Titles
Meet Me at Sunset
This Christmas

Oyster Bay Series
Feels Like Home
Along Came You
Maybe This Time
This Thing Called Love
Those Summer Nights
Still the One
One Fine Day
Had to Be You

Misty Point Series
One Week to the Wedding
The Winter Wedding Plan

Sweeter in the City Series
Sweeter in the Summer
Sweeter Than Sunshine
No Sweeter Love
One Sweet Christmas

Briar Creek Series
Mistletoe on Main Street
A Match Made on Main Street
Hope Springs on Main Street
Love Blooms on Main Street
Christmas Comes to Main Street

Harlequin Special Edition
'Twas the Week Before Christmas
Recipe for Romance

Copyright © 2021 by Megan Leavell
ISBN 978-1-7346208-5-6

All rights reserved. No part of this publication may be reproduced, distributed or transmitted in any form or by any means, without prior written permission.

Publisher's Note: This is a work of fiction. Names, characters, places, and incidents are a product of the author's imagination. Locales and public names are sometimes used for atmospheric purposes. Any resemblance to actual people, living or dead, or to businesses, companies, events, institutions, or locales is completely coincidental.

Return to Me

1

Brooke Conway had a secret.

A couple of them, really, not that she was particularly proud. The most pressing one was that she was back in Blue Harbor, her hometown, and even though she'd let her sisters and parents know of her plans, they hadn't known that plans had changed. That instead of arriving in town today, she'd actually been here for four whole days. Laying low. Fighting that pull in her chest that said coming here was a bad idea.

It hadn't been easy to pull off, exactly, not when her new apartment was located smack in the middle of Main Street, for all to see. She'd changed her flight, flagged a cab, fought back the apprehension as each mile ticked by, bringing her closer to the northern Michigan coast. She'd waited in the cab for a full ten minutes in case she'd been spotted, shielded behind sunglasses and happy that the inexpensive moving company she'd hired wouldn't be delivering most of her belongings until the following week, so she didn't have to worry about carrying too much, or drawing attention with a big unloading day. Not that she had much. In Manhattan, she was rarely in her apartment. Other than a few pieces of furniture and boxes of dishes that served as mere trays for her take-out containers, she didn't own much other than fabric, and her most prized possession, the thing she had invested in and couldn't live without, her state of the art, industrial-grade sewing machine, she had managed to take with her, though not without paying dearly for its transport, and even then she had fretted as she'd sipped her diet soda and stared out the small oval window at the clouds, hoping that it hadn't gotten lost in transit, only exhaling when she saw it coming down the cargo line in baggage claim.

This she'd carried up the stairs, as carefully as others might hold a newborn baby.

The apartment was semi-furnished with a guest bed in the second room, a small sofa in the living room, and a kitchen table and chairs near the front bay window. She'd set her sewing machine on the table, retrieved grocery bags with darting eyes, and then made one final trip for her suitcase and tote, tipping the driver handsomely for allowing her to stop off at the big supermarket near the airport along the way. Once the door was locked behind her, she'd pulled all the blinds. And that was how she had stayed for the past four days. Hiding in her own hometown.

Maybe there was no excuse. Maybe it was shameful. But coming back had been difficult enough—staying wouldn't be easier, but she'd gotten over the hurdle, dove headfirst, like she used to do in the icy waters of the lake on the first warm day. Eventually, she'd get used to things. Acclimate. Eventually, it would all be okay. So she told herself. When the cab had driven over the town line, she'd immediately questioned her decision, causing her heart to speed up and her mind to spin and a hundred excuses to turn right around, even though U-turns were possibly illegal in Michigan (she hadn't been back in so long, she couldn't be sure) and she was fairly certain that the driver was losing patience.

But there was nowhere to go back to, and that was the reason she pressed on, quietly moved into the space that she'd rented on Main Street—a vacant storefront for her wedding dress boutique and a small apartment conveniently above—even though her sister Gabby's flower shop was only a block down and several of her cousins were within reach, too.

She just needed…a moment. She needed to settle in, catch her breath, and find her footing. Her family would see plenty of her going forward. She was back now.

Back. Just thinking of that made the knot tighten in her stomach, even though she knew it was the right choice. Not that she'd had much of one. Losing her job in New York had seen to that. And the fashion industry was competitive, something that had been a reality check from the start. For nearly six years she had worked hard to get ahead, trying to live her dream. Living a glamorous life, some might say, even if it had become an empty one.

She missed her sisters. And her cousins, who were so much closer than friends. And her parents. And this town. And…No. That was all she missed.

Or so she told herself every time her blood pressure surged and she wondered if she should have held out a little longer, interviewed a bit more in New York, hoped that something would come along.

Except that something had come along. An opportunity of a lifetime, really. A chance to finally have her own line. Right here in Blue Harbor.

But oh, just thinking about her shop sent a flutter through her heart straight down to her stomach and she felt a swell of hope as she imagined all its possibilities. She'd fine-tuned her skills over the years, learned from the best, but now she had the opportunity to make something of her own.

It was a small dream, perhaps. After all, a custom wedding dress shop in Blue Harbor was a far cry from an atelier in Paris or Manhattan. But it was her dream, and she had found a way to make it come true.

No need to mention that she was also running away. For the second time in her life.

But this was different, she reminded herself. This time she was coming home. This time she had a plan that she could stick to...

Well, almost. It was the almost part that nagged her. The part about the loan she'd need to apply for if she wanted to grow things the way that she'd envisioned—to hire an assistant, take out advertising space in magazines, and get her name out there, at least on a regional level. She'd avoided loans for years, choosing to rent rather than buy in New York, and luckily not needing a car when she was there, but this time she owed it to herself to take a risk, to borrow against her future.

For now, she had a few more hours of work ahead of her before she headed over to her parents' home, where her family insisted on having a party to welcome her officially. By now, they would know she was back, or at least arriving at any minute. She could picture her mother standing at the window, her hands gripping each other, wondering if she should pop over into town to see if her middle daughter needed help. Brooke's father would advise her to wait, to let Brooke settle in on her own time. Her mother would probably then mention she needed something at the store. Find an excuse to linger in town a bit. Maybe stroll down Main; it was such a lovely spring day and all…

Brooke turned to the window of her apartment and parted the wooden blinds just wide enough to look down onto Main Street. The blossoming eaves of the trees shielded most of the view, but still, she was relieved to see that the sidewalks were full of strangers only, young families on their way to a late lunch, or perhaps hoping to catch the next ferry out to Evening Island, where they could rent bikes and ride laps around the small island, hoping to catch sight of some early lilacs in bloom.

Still, she knew her mother, and she knew that she wouldn't patiently wait for the clock to strike five o'clock when Gabby closed her flower shop and promised to personally escort Brooke to their childhood home. Just the two of them, she'd said over the phone. Like the old days.

Meaning the days when Brooke was still single.

She'd tried to block that time from her mind. A big wedding. So much planning, and effort, and fanfare.

And then…Well, no use in thinking about what came after that. It was ancient history. She was a grown woman now. An independent woman. A woman with her own business, a lease, and a family that loved her. A family that couldn't wait to welcome her tonight. She didn't know why she was dreading it, but a part of her did. Because this party would make it official. Life in Blue Harbor. And even though she was back in town, she wasn't quite ready for the feeling of such permanency just yet.

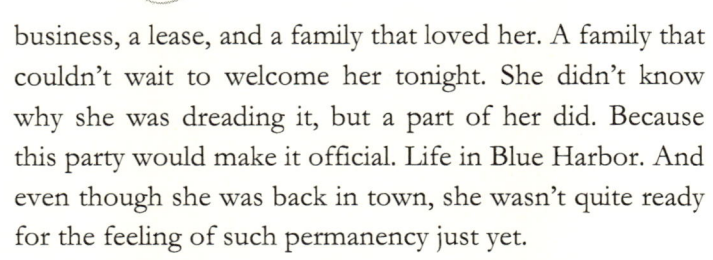

Happy that she'd bought enough groceries to pack her fridge and the second shelf of the small pantry, she made herself a mug of instant coffee and slathered peanut butter on a slice of bread as a late lunch. There would be plenty of time for proper food once she was ready to go out in public, but today she planned to get the finishing touches made on her storefront, maybe even set up her back office, too.

With her sandwich only half-eaten, she took the stairs down to the street level, let herself in the back door with the key that the landlord had left under the mat—a telling sign that she was back in Blue Harbor if ever there was one—and entered the storage room, which was luckily clean and tidy, and painted the same shade of light blue as the other walls of the space. It had been easier that way, giving direction from afar, to have everything painted the same color, though she might change her small office later, to something more distinctive yet feminine, like a soft blush or an elegant lavender. It would be her personal space, where she would do all her alterations and sewing, and right next to the closet that would soon hold bolts of the prettiest fabrics that she'd collected over the years, from lace to chiffon to rich satins that she never tired of working with, however heavy the ballgowns sometimes became. Back in New York, her vision was credited to her boss. Her designs were tweaked to suit someone else's vision. Someone else's success. Now, she had the power to create anything and everything she wanted.

And that...well, that alone was a reason to come back here.

And do what it took to secure that loan.

Inside the storefront, the light fixtures were in dire need of replacing, but she had put off making a call to a handyman until today, knowing how quickly the word would spread if she'd scheduled him any sooner. Old Gus would tell her dad down at the docks by noon, she was sure. The men in town sat out on their boats as often as the weather permitted, under the guise of baiting whitefish in Lake Huron, even though most of the wives suspected it was an excuse for them to get out of the house—not that anyone was complaining. Since Brooke's father's retirement from the family's orchard and winery, he spent nearly as much time fishing as he did traveling.

Only her parents weren't traveling now. Nope. They'd been sure to tell her that they didn't have another trip planned for months. They were all hers.

She wasn't sure how she felt about that.

She made a note in her planner that Gus would be arriving the next morning. With any luck, he could get the fixtures replaced while she hung the mirrors and set up the dressing rooms, in case she needed a hand with any of those tasks. The shop had once belonged to Patsy, and it was conveniently a former women's clothing boutique—one that Brooke had worked at not so long ago, even if it felt like another lifetime. When Gabby had mentioned that Patsy was closing up shop, Brooke saw an opportunity that she knew might not come along again for a while. She'd hung up the phone with her sister, paced her shoebox of an apartment in Manhattan, and then, with a shaking hand, dialed Patsy herself and asked about taking over the lease.

Two weeks later, here she was. Standing in the space she had slowly transformed. Making it all her own.

She stood back and marveled at the sight. Some people might think it was ironic that she was a wedding dress designer.

One person in particular, she thought, flicking off the light.

*

At four forty-five, Brooke decided it was safe to venture outside. Still, this was Blue Harbor; the population was small. The one time she'd visited since leaving, she'd been sure to stay at her parents' house and never leave. And as eager as she was to see her family now, to know that at the end of the street was her cousin Cora's holiday shop, and just off Main was the café that her cousin Amelia now owned and the new bakery run by her cousin Maddie, she also knew that she could pace herself. She had all weekend to visit them. And next week, too. Next month. Next year. She wasn't going anywhere this time. She was putting down roots.

And speaking of, some flowers were needed to flank her glossy black paned door. Something seasonal yet elegant, she thought. She made a mental note to talk to Gabby about it tonight as she stood back to study the storefront from a distance. The front bay window was covered by a gauzy white curtain, and her sign was yet to be installed, covering the ghost of Patsy's, which had left a discoloration mark on the brick in its removal.

The sign was scheduled for delivery tomorrow—she'd triple checked and was tracking it by phone—and she'd already started to dream about her opening week window display. Something springy, yet elegant. Maybe with a garland of fresh blooms framing the glass?

She turned at a tap on her shoulder, expecting to see her sister.

"There you are!" she exclaimed with a smile until she caught the mischievous gleam of a man—and not just of any man. "I mean…you. I…I didn't mean you."

Kyle Harrison stared back at her, his expression somewhere between confusion and amusement. Immediately, Brooke stiffened. She knew she'd have to face him. Prepared for it, even. Rehearsed it over and over until she almost lost her courage to leave New York at all. But she hadn't expected it to happen the very first day she ventured outside. Darn small-town life.

"Brooke." He looked her up and down, making her pleased that she'd dressed up for tonight's family party in her best jeans, wedge heels, blousy top, and gold necklace to match her earrings. She'd had her hair trimmed and highlighted before leaving the big city—really, sometimes she thought the person she would miss the most in her old life was Felix in the East Village salon that didn't look like much from the front, but worked magic on the inside.

Not that she should care what Kyle thought of her appearance. He was a part of her past; only now, she saw that he had changed in the years since she'd been back. His face had thinned out, and fine lines had appeared around his eyes. Always lanky and moderately tall, he'd filled out in the shoulders and chest.

Not that she was noticing.

But one thing was the same. That steady blue gaze. She tried to look away, but the pull was too strong.

"Kyle." She was an adult. Thirty-one years old, meaning no excuses. No sense in making this awkward, especially now that she was going to be living in town. "This is a surprise."

He cocked an eyebrow. She'd nearly forgotten how he could do that so expertly, with just one brow. "Surprise? You're the one back in the town I never left. The surprise is on me."

She couldn't tell by his expression what he truly meant by that word, but she decided that it didn't matter. She and Kyle hadn't meant anything to each other since they were kids.

Another untruth, she thought. One she'd tried to tell herself.

But one thing was very true. This was the town that Kyle had never left. Refused to leave, more like it. And that was something that she didn't need to be reminded about because she had never forgotten it, or forgiven him.

"I assumed word would have traveled by now," she said pleasantly. They both knew how the gossip mill ran in this town, and Patsy was a willing participant. "I'm opening a shop." She didn't go into further detail. He'd lost the right to know about her life a long time ago.

He glanced at the old clothing shop as if only now placing her connection to it. His gaze slid back to her, and if she didn't know better, she'd say he was frowning. "So you've moved back then? You're not just visiting?"

"Nope," she said, slapping her hands at her hips. "I mean, yep. I mean, I'm...I'm here to stay."

The frown that pulled at his brow was noticeable, and she released a shaky breath. She looked down the street in the direction of Gabby's flower shop. Seriously, where was her sister?

Maybe she should start walking in that direction. Chances were that Gabby would be pulling up at any minute, or she'd pass her on her walk. There was plenty she could say to Kyle (and plenty that she wanted to say, oh yes), but now wasn't the time.

She glanced back at Kyle. His brown hair was still wavy, cut a little shorter than it was last time she'd seen him. He was wearing a blue tee-shirt that brought out the color of his eyes. Brought out some nicely defined muscles in those arms, too, she thought, then quickly darted her gaze back up to his face.

So he looked good. Lots of men did. It didn't mean she got all girly and weird about it. Besides, she had a new shop to run and dresses to make, appointments to book. Now wasn't the time for a relationship.

Especially not with Kyle of all people. She'd made that mistake once in her life. Had a marriage certificate to prove it, too.

A vehicle honked and Brooke jumped, almost forgetting that she had been out here for a purpose, waiting for her sister, who was now waving through the window, a big smile on her face that slipped only slightly when Kyle turned and waved back.

"That's my ride," Brooke said, moving toward the street.

"Guess there's no sense in saying good-bye, now that you're here to stay," Kyle said, accentuating her words. His look was appraising as she reached for the handle to Gabby's flower delivery van. "But then, I don't seem to recall you saying good-bye last time I saw you, either."

Brooke pinched her lips and pulled open the door. Leave it to Kyle to remember that detail and leave out the rest, like the reason she'd left him to begin with. She fought back the words that threatened to spill, her heart speeding up with a fresh wave and frustration that only Kyle could spark in her.

She pushed it back, reminded herself that it was in the past. That there was nothing left to talk to Kyle about—well, except one thing. She'd need to stay on his good side if she wanted that loan to come through, so she forced a tight smile and said, "I'm sure we'll see each other soon."

It was a guarantee, living in a town this small, and one she had known coming back here.

But sliding into the seat and being pulled in for a hug by her sister reminded her that this was why she'd come back, that her family was worth it. And that Kyle meant nothing at all.

2

Kyle pushed through the door of Harrison's Pub and walked straight to the bar. The anchor-shaped clock on the shiplap wall said it was four minutes past five. Not that he needed an excuse. Brooke Conway was back in town, and the words straight from her mouth were that she was here to stay, and that...Well, that called for more than a beer on tap.

He pulled a shot glass from the shelf under the bar, filled it with whiskey, and knocked it back, letting it burn his throat.

"Whoa there," he heard someone chuckle. He glowered at his older brother, whose amusement at his misfortune was hardly appreciated. "Bad day?"

Kyle raised an eyebrow but didn't elaborate. Ryan would hear soon enough. Everyone would. And then everyone would be looking at him, watching him, waiting for a reaction, a story to share over a pint.

He wasn't going to give them one. So Brooke was back in town. They'd gone their separate ways coming up on six years now. Yes, he could state the exact amount of time, without really needing to stop and calculate it, but why harp on the past?

Even if the past had just become the present.

"We need to discuss your plans for the menu," Kyle said instead. He rinsed the shot glass and set it upside down on the mat to dry, eager to change the subject, and not just to ward off a deeper investigation from his brother. He needed to focus on something he could make sense of, not let his mind trail to things—and people—that he'd rather forget.

"Finally seeing things my way?" Ryan looked downright boastful. With their four-year age gap, Ryan was still of the impression that he held some authority over his younger brother, even if Kyle had been the one running this pub single-handedly, and doing a fine enough job of it, too.

"I told you," Kyle said, exasperated. "I like the menu the way it is. And so does everyone else. And you'd know that if you had been around here all these years."

"Still blaming me for getting a real job, huh?"

Kyle shot him a warning look and Ryan had the sense to look almost regretful. This was an argument they'd had many times. Too many. And they never got anywhere. Even as kids, Ryan was the one who focused on facts and numbers and Kyle was the one who was always sketching, stretching his mind to come up with new ideas. Their differences grew along with them, with Ryan going into business and Kyle...ending up here. From the way things were going tonight, nothing was going to change anytime soon. Not between them.

And not with this bar.

Kyle supposed he should count his victories rather than take issue with the old wounds that had a way of opening up every time that he and Ryan had talked over the years, and even more so now that Ryan was back in town. And hell-bent on sticking his nose in the family business. Judging by the way Ryan slung a rag over his shoulder and stalked to the other side of the long bar, the idea that Kyle could have some hidden personal secret seemed to have been forgotten.

Normally Ryan's insistence to change up the pub they'd inherited from their father, and his father before that, was a source of frustration to Kyle. Kyle liked things the way they were.

Always had, he thought ruefully.

He pushed his mind away from Brooke.

"You know I didn't push you to come back and take over," he said with a heavy sigh. What he didn't say was that he'd wanted to, just as much as he couldn't bring himself to do that. His father loved his old place, much more than Kyle ever would or could, but Ryan wouldn't give it the justice it deserved, and the fact that he already had an established life somewhere else at the time was only a convenient excuse.

"The menu is old and tired, just like this place," Ryan said.

"It was Dad's menu, and as I said, the people like it." Kyle could hear the same old resentment creeping into his tone, and he checked himself.

"If they like it so much, then why does the Carriage House always have a bigger crowd?"

"A different crowd," Kyle corrected, thinking of the posh and cozy pub in the back of the quaint Main Street inn that attracted locals looking for a social spot and tourists hoping for something authentic yet upscale. "Dad never cared about that scene."

"Dad isn't here anymore," Ryan said, not unkindly. They fell silent for a moment. There was a loud burst of laughter from the guys near the window. The television screen seemed especially loud.

"Well, Dad entrusted the place to me," Kyle said firmly.

"To us." Ryan squared him with a look.

"Yeah? Well, nice of you to finally make an appearance." Kyle hated this, the arguing, almost as much as he hated the fact that his brother wasn't completely wrong. He'd been running this place for years now, or keeping it going at least. And his brother had bigger hopes for it. Bigger ideas. He didn't know who was right anymore. He just knew that he'd had enough change for one lifetime.

"I have an objective opinion," Ryan said firmly. "You need to take a step back and look at what's going on here. You're too close to it to see that you're not doing the business any help by not changing with the times."

"Why don't you go back to your office job in Cleveland and leave the pub to me?" Kyle asked.

"Because I missed the view of the water. Because I was bored, and life was passing me by."

"Because your girlfriend dumped you," Kyle teased, even though he knew it was the other way around, or at least, mutual.

"That's rich, coming from you," Ryan said, and even though it was their usual brotherly banter, Kyle couldn't help but feel the sting, especially after just seeing Brooke.

Brooke. Back in town. He still couldn't believe it. Just like he couldn't believe how good it felt to see her again, to see the light in her eyes, and the lift of her smile. And her voice. He'd nearly forgotten it, or tried to, at least.

He'd thought he was over her. But, then, he'd thought a lot of things. And how had that all turned out?

*

Brooke's parents were already waiting for her on the front porch when Gabby pulled onto the gravel driveway lined with happy yellow tulips. Her younger sister Jenna shot up from the steps and bolted across the yard, her ponytail made her seem more youthful than her age. Even though she'd come to visit New York a couple of times, Brooke still couldn't believe how much Jenna had changed. She was a young woman now, well into her twenties. An adult with a music career and an apartment of her own. And oh, how Brooke had missed her. She'd missed all of them; she just hadn't let herself feel that way until now.

"You're here, you're really here!" That was her mother, of course, pulling her into her arms, her scent so familiar that tears prickled the backs of Brooke's eyes.

"I'm here, Mom," Brooke promised. "To stay."

"Oh, let me look at you." Miriam pushed her away only long enough to give her a good once-over. "Is it a requirement in New York to be so skinny?"

"Maybe in the fashion industry," Gabby said, jumping to her defense. She gave her a little wink. "Besides, I think you look beautiful. I will be borrowing those jeans, by the way."

Brooke laughed and gave her father a long hug. Swapping clothes with her sisters was a small perk that she'd nearly forgotten about. Being the middle sister, she usually had the best of both worlds, but now that they were all grown and roughly the same size, it would be even easier.

"When do your things arrive?" her mother asked as she looped her arm through Brooke's and led her up to the house.

"Monday," Brooke said.

"Well, let me know if you need any help."

Help. Another perk of being home. She'd gotten used to doing everything on her own, not depending on anyone, not trusting anyone either.

"Considering what I paid the moving company, I'm hoping they can handle most of it. And there's not much to unpack. Mostly just a bed and sofa and some linens and clothes. And fabric, of course." She'd been collecting it for years, never able to resist something that caught her eye, even if she didn't have a purpose for it in that moment. But now, she did.

"You and your fabric." Her mother laughed. "Even when you were little, you were always cutting up old clothes, sometimes before I had a chance to pass them down to Jenna!"

They all turned to Jenna, forever good-natured, who shrugged and smiled. "I never minded."

Now their mother gave her youngest daughter a tight squeeze. "I'm sorry, honey."

"There's nothing to be sorry for, Mom. Besides, I got a lot of good stuff. Brooke always had expensive taste."

Brooke laughed. "And I always took care of my things. Speaking of..." She looked at her parents hopefully. "You don't by any chance still have my old bike in the garage?"

Her father looked pleased. "Of course we do! Might have a few cobwebs on it, but I'll go out and dust it off myself. Should fit easily into the back of Gabby's van."

Brooke felt her shoulders relax. With Blue Harbor being so small, it was customary for locals to ride their bikes from spring through fall, until the first snow fell. Tourists rented bikes and often took them out on the ferry to Evening Island, where no cars were allowed. She hadn't needed a car in New York, of course, and she wasn't in the position to be investing in such a large purchase right now.

"Are the cousins coming?" she asked. She had seven in town in total, all girls. There were the four Conway girls, whose father was Uncle Dennis, her father's brother, and then there were the three Clark girls, on her mother's side.

"No, we thought it would be just us tonight," her mother explained, as they entered the house.

"We wanted you all to ourselves," Gabby chimed in.

Brooke was glad to hear it. It would help her ease in, even though she'd gotten the worst part of her return over and done with already. The reason she'd dreaded returning. The reason she'd stayed away.

The reason she'd left to begin with.

But all those uncomfortable feelings went away as soon as she stepped foot into the front hall of the old Colonial she had lived in for the better part of her life. Home. She was home. She would know it with her eyes closed, by the smell of the lemon-scented soap her mother used to wash the floors, and the hint of basil from the herbs that she grew on the kitchen windowsill.

She took it all in, even though it was exactly as she'd left it. The same pictures hung on the wall. The same coat rack stood in the corner. The same stairs with the landing and the big picture window where her mother hung a giant wreath each year during the holiday season.

"I've forgotten how beautiful this place is," she breathed.

Her mother chuckled, but her smile was proud. "Please, it's getting run down. The water heater went out this winter and we'll need to replace the doors soon."

"Not the one where you carved our heights?" Brooke asked in alarm, not sure how that suddenly came back to her. Each year, on their birthday, Steve Conway would get out the measuring stick and call them over.

Her father shook his head. "No one will ever touch those doorframes. I wouldn't even let Gus touch up the trim."

Brooke smiled. "Well, it smells delicious."

"All your favorites, of course!" Her mother beamed. "You girls settle in and I'll finish up. I thought we could eat on the porch tonight? It's warm, and I have sweaters if the breeze picks up."

Of course, she had sweaters, because that's how she was. Nurturing, caring, always there when Brooke had needed her. She could have trusted her mother with any news, but for some reason, she couldn't bring herself to share everything, maybe because she didn't want to disappoint her further. She could still never forget the look in her parents' eyes when she'd told them she had left Kyle.

Her mother had tried to talk her out of it, encouraged her to give it time, but Brooke, for maybe the first time in her life, hadn't wanted to listen to her mother's advice, and her mother had known not to press the topic.

Relationships take work, was all she said. But she'd said something else too. Something that had been a blessing of sorts: *Follow your heart.*

Gabby waited until they had settled in the living room before giving her a coy smile. Brooke had been sure to keep her too busy chatting about all the other news in town on the ride over for her sister to have a chance to bring Kyle up sooner, but Brooke knew that it was coming. Still, she braced herself.

"So...how was it seeing Kyle?"

Jenna's eyes burst open as she leaned forward. "You already saw Kyle? How's that for bad luck?"

Brooke darted her eyes to the doorway, but from the clamoring going on in the kitchen, she knew it was safe to assume they couldn't be overheard.

Just in case, she lowered her voice. "I bumped into him on the street when I came out to wait for Gabby."

She shrugged, trying to keep her tone light. "It was inevitable, wasn't it?"

"You seem okay with it." Gabby's look was guarded, as if she were waiting for Brooke to break into tears at any point, or stir up old arguments that she had once confided in her sisters.

Brooke sighed and let her gaze fall on the collection of framed photos her mother kept on the built-in bookcases. She gave a small smile, looking back at the best moments of her youth. There was one of them all lined up in front of their pumpkins at the orchard, and another of them all sitting under the Christmas tree. There was one of Jenna at the piano that was sitting at the opposite end of the room, and another of Gabby holding a big bouquet of flowers she'd picked from the yard.

Brooke realized with a start that there was one photo missing—it was her engagement photo. The one that used to be kept in an etched silver frame beside the one of her parents...

But, of course, it would be gone. Long gone. Even though her parents had held out hope that she and Kyle would patch things up, as soon as she decided to leave town and pursue her career, they had accepted the fact that it wouldn't happen. Since then, she never asked about Kyle and they never mentioned him. They all knew well enough that if she wanted an update, she would ask, and she had refrained, even when some days, like on their wedding anniversary each year, she did start to wonder.

She looked back to her sisters, who were watching her expectantly. "There's nothing to say. Kyle and I haven't been a part of each other's lives in a very long time." She couldn't resist the opportunity to find out a little information now, though, just so she was prepared. Back in New York, she had the luxury of not knowing the details of his life, but here in Blue Harbor, she would eventually find out. Best to get it over with from the start. Best to know what she was dealing with, too.

She fiddled with the strap at the back of her shoes, hoping to look casual. "He's still at the pub?"

The pub had been a sore spot, might have even been the root cause of their breakup, some might say, but she knew that it ran deeper than that. Kyle did too. He'd been happy to settle down in the small town they'd lived in all their lives, and she...well, she wanted more, she supposed.

"Yep. And it's exactly as you remember it," Jenna said.

In other words, a local joint that catered more to the beer-drinking, sport-watching, middle-aged men in town. The food had never been the appeal, and most patrons went to have a few drinks, share a few laughs, and shoot pool.

It was dark. It was dated. And it was depressing.

And chances were, it was a money pit.

"I'm a little surprised it hasn't gone out of business yet," Brooke murmured. With tourism being such a large part of Blue Harbor's economy, the restaurant scene was competitive and lively, and Harrison's had never pulled in many out-of-town guests.

"They have their regulars, of course," Jenna said with a wrinkle of her nose.

Gabby nodded. "But Ryan's back now. I think for good."

Brooke idly wondered how that would work out. Kyle and Ryan had always butted heads growing up, even if Ryan was an all-around nice guy.

Like his brother. Kyle was a fundamentally nice guy. Hometown guy. Small-town guy. The only guy she'd ever known when she married him.

"Ryan's helping at the pub?" She blinked rapidly, thinking of the irony of it all. She finally returned to Blue Harbor, just when Kyle might be free to leave it?

"That's what I hear..." Gabby shrugged to show that she didn't have any more information to share.

"You're frowning," Jenna noted.

Brooke perked up, forcing a smile. "Just tired is all."

Gabby nodded in understanding. "It's a long trip. And all that traveling today!"

Brooke shifted uncomfortably in her chair. She was eager to get back to the conversation about Kyle and Ryan. "Ryan never showed an interest in the pub before."

"I hear he's looking to make some improvements," Gabby said.

"Not if your husband has his way—" Jenna started and then stopped. She winced. "Sorry, I meant ex-husband."

Brooke waved a hand dismissively through the air, showing no offense. Because the truth of the matter was that Jenna hadn't said anything wrong. She'd actually been right.

Kyle was still her husband, in the legal sense of the word.

And that was something no one else needed to know.

3

The cousins had all decided to meet up on Saturday night, something that Gabby had organized, not that Brooke was complaining. They were meeting at the Carriage House Inn Pub—not only because it had always been one of their favorite spots in town but also, Brooke knew, because the chances of seeing Kyle there were remote.

Still, as she entered the cozy restaurant, flanked by Jenna and Gabby who had met her at her new apartment, deemed it had potential, and then insisted that she change from the black sundress to something more "appropriate," Brooke darted her eyes over the room nervously, only feeling her shoulders relax when she didn't immediately spot Kyle anywhere.

And why should she? He ran the local watering hole. He would be working. Tucked away behind another set of doors, probably pouring beers and calling out orders over the raucous near the pool table. Nothing for her to worry about. This was going to be a girls' night, a long time coming, and a perk to being back in town that she intended to enjoy.

"Were you this uptight in New York?" Gabby gave her a funny smile as they slid into a table near the big windows that were pulled open to let the breeze pass. It was a warm night for spring, but it was the kind of night that Brooke had longed for in the city, where the city noises and smells had made her crave the fresh air that she could feel all the way into her lungs when she breathed. Quiet nights, where she could hear the water lapping at the shore, or the crickets chirping. Or, on the clearest of them all, a glimpse of the Northern Lights, turning the canvas of the night sky into a beautiful work of art.

"Who said I'm uptight?" Brooke remarked. It was true, though, that she wasn't the same carefree young girl, and she didn't just have her time in the city to blame for it. The life she'd planned on had gone awry, and now, she took extra care in being as prepared as possible for anything that could come her way.

"Ever since we left your apartment you've looked like you're waiting for someone to jump out of the bushes!" Gabby laughed. "Relax! This isn't Manhattan."

It was nowhere near Manhattan, and Brooke didn't feel like pointing out that she'd feel less twitchy walking through the city streets alone than down Main Street in Blue Harbor. Here, everyone knew her story. Or at least, most of it. And back in New York, the only person who gave her anxiety was her boss.

Another person who hadn't believed in her enough to commit to the long haul.

"I am relaxed," she insisted, giving them both a forced smile.

A burst of deep, gravelly laughter made her stiffen, and her eyes roamed to the bar, unable to part with thoughts of Kyle against her better judgment. But it was Jackson Bradford. Handsome as ever. And a crowd of people she half recognized from growing up and the rest probably falling under the tourist category. "I'm back in my element. Honestly, it feels like I never left."

That statement held far too much truth. Ever since running into Kyle, she couldn't completely shake him from her head. All those memories she had tried to push away were fighting to come back. When she left town, she'd been his wife. She'd loved him. She'd...

She'd been broken-hearted, she reminded herself.

"You tried to wear a little black dress out for drinks tonight," Jenna said gently.

"You can never go wrong with a little black dress," Brooke told her. But then, you couldn't go wrong with great jeans and a black top like she had worn instead, either.

Gabby raised an eyebrow and pulled the drinks menu closer. "You can in Blue Harbor. This is a resort town. It's casual. It's slow-paced." She gave her a mock stern look across the table. "Clearly, you've been gone too long."

"Well, I'm back now," Brooke said. But Gabby was right. There was no use for half of her wardrobe here in her hometown, where jeans and tees, or capris and tanks, or cotton sundresses paired with flip-flops would do. A little black dress might come in handy for a date.

Not that she'd be having one of those anytime soon.

"So," she said, after glancing at the cocktail list and deciding on a glass of white wine—the family brand, of course. Like many establishments in town, locals supported each other, and the Bradfords and Conways went way back. "Tell me everything I've missed." Last night their conversation had been somewhat suppressed by their parents, centering on safe topics like the weather, her parents' future trips, and her Uncle Dennis's upcoming wedding.

The juicy topics had been shelved, and even though she talked with her sisters regularly, she wanted to be sure she was caught up on everything once her cousins arrived.

"Well, you know that Robbie and Britt are back together," Gabby said. No doubt that Robbie Bradford would eventually marry Britt, too, finally uniting the two families officially.

"And Amelia and Matt," Jenna added. Another Bradford, seeing as Matt was Robbie's cousin.

"And Maddie is now dating Cole McCarthy," Gabby said, widening her eyes. "The biggest surprise of them all."

"Nope." Jenna shook her head. "The biggest surprise is Cora. She's very close with a man who just moved here over the winter. He's a single father. Very handsome."

"And his daughter is adorable," Gabby said with a sigh. "That leaves the three of us. Single."

Single. Brooke let that word fall on silence. While she had considered herself single since the day she'd left Kyle and this town, and she assumed that Kyle did, too, she was legally anything but single.

"Well, and all our other cousins are still single, too?" Brooke gave her a smile of encouragement. She knew that

Gabby's love life was a disappointment to her. It came from delivering one too many arrangements on Valentine's Day and not receiving enough for herself over the years.

"Yep!" Jenna brightened and waved over her shoulder. "And here comes one right now. Over here, Bella!"

Brooke stood up to greet her cousin, pulling her into a long hug, chatting excitedly about the new shop and all of her plans for it. Isabella owned the bookstore in town, and before they had even sat down, she had insisted that Brooke attend the next book club meeting.

"I won't take no for an answer," Bella said. "Besides, it will be a good opportunity for you to spread the word about your new business. Everyone must know someone who is getting married."

Gabby nodded. "I'm happy to keep a stack of your cards on my counter. Most brides-to-be at least come through to get a quote from me when it comes to their bouquets and centerpieces."

"You're being modest," Bella chided. "We all know that you are the most popular florist in the county for weddings."

Gabby blushed but didn't argue.

"And I occasionally play at weddings," Jenna offered. Like Gabby, she was playing down her musical talents, as well as her demand. Brooke knew full well that being asked to lead the Christmas Choir was a major accomplishment, but that Jenna was just happy to be doing something she loved.

Brooke could relate to that.

"There's always someone who catches the bouquet, next in line. I can hand them your card along with mine."

"I still need to get those made," Brooke thought, now wishing that she'd brought a tote bag large enough to hold her planner, even though her cross-body purse looked so much better with her outfit.

She could hear her boss now. How could someone so creative be so rigid?

For many reasons, Brooke thought.

"When is your opening?" Bella wanted to know.

"The moving company arrives Monday, and I'm hoping to have everything set up by Wednesday. It will be a soft opening, no big party or announcement or anything." The last thing she needed was to draw more attention to herself. She'd gotten used to a private life in Manhattan. She'd gotten used to being alone.

"Well, between you and Gabby, you'll have the market covered just in time for wedding season!" Jenna was clearly happy for her, and Brooke was grateful for it. Still, her nerves fluttered when she thought of all that she still had to do…and what she had done. That she was here. That she was going to open her own shop. And hope that someone would actually buy something.

Tempering expectations, she said, "Oh, most spring brides have probably already picked out their gowns by now, but some summer weddings, maybe."

"Wedding season." Gabby looked wistful. "Is it crazy to think that I'm always the one making the bouquets and never the one catching them?"

Brooke patted her hand. "Eventually the odds will be in your favor."

"What's this I hear about weddings?" Britt and Cora appeared at the table, both happy to bend down and greet Brooke with a hug.

"I hear you're back together with Robbie," Brooke said to Britt once everyone had settled into chairs. "Any wedding bells in the future?"

Britt's lips thinned. "The only bells I've been hearing are the ringing in my ears when Candy starts practicing the song she wants to sing for my dad at their reception."

The entire table laughed. Even though Brooke had never met the woman who was going to be marrying her Uncle Dennis, she'd heard enough about her to form a vivid picture. Slightly younger, eager to please, and a personality that couldn't be topped.

"Where are Amelia and Maddie?" she asked, eager to see the other two Conway sisters.

"They'll be here once Amelia closes up the café," Britt said.

"Heidi and Natalie should be here any minute too," Bella chimed in. Like the others, she kept tabs on her sisters, remaining as close with them in her adult years as they'd been as children. She motioned to the bar, where Jackson was pouring drinks, just as he was doing the last time Brooke was here, years ago. "I'll get this round."

Happily, they all told her their orders, most of which consisted of white wine.

"Look at us," Brooke said with a sigh. "All out on a Saturday night. All grown up."

"Not that much has changed," Gabby said. "None of us are married. Yet," she added, flashing a look in Britt's direction.

Brooke saw her cousin's cheeks turn pink, but it was Cora whose eyes widened in horror. "Well, Brooke *was* married," she corrected Gabby gently.

Gabby gave Brooke a guilty smile. "I'm sorry, hon. It was so long ago, and we're used to seeing Kyle around as…"

"A single guy?" Brooke didn't know why the thought of it caused a knot to form in her stomach. After all, she'd dated a bit in New York.

Her heart sped up as she waited for one of the women to answer that question because she wasn't so sure that she wanted to hear what they had to say.

They'd been each other's first loves. Too young for anything more serious beforehand, too content to think about ever taking a break and testing the waters. But now they'd been apart, hadn't even spoken, living separate lives. Single lives.

She swallowed hard, pushing back the urge to inquire about Kyle's romantic status, and brightened when Bella reappeared at the table, juggling three glasses of wine in two hands, and the topic was forgotten.

"Jackson's right behind me with the rest," Bella said, just as he appeared.

He grinned at them all, his gaze landing on Brooke. "Well, I'll be. Brooke Conway. I thought I saw you sitting over here. What brings you back to town after all this time?"

"I moved back," she replied, again surprised that news hadn't traveled by now. Her family didn't tend to gossip, but considering that she'd rented space from Patsy, she had half expected welcoming signs to parade her into town.

"Whoa. Does Kyle know?" Jackson was older than Kyle by a few years, but they'd always been friendly, and Brooke assumed more so as they'd aged, even if they did technically run competing operations. The nice thing about Blue Harbor was that tourism was such a big draw that the pubs were rarely in need of business, and on the off season, the locals were loyal patrons. There weren't many places to hunker down in the brutal winter months when the snow hit and stayed and the lake effect wind made you want to stay inside and never leave.

The pub of the Carriage House Inn had been around for generations, and so had the smaller establishment owned by the Harrisons, though theirs was solely a restaurant and bar, not one of the many white wood framed inns that lined Main Street.

Gabby swatted Jackson painfully.

"It's okay," Brooke assured them. Everyone had a past. "And yes, he does know. I bumped into him yesterday."

The amusement in Jackson's eyes told her that he was eager to ask how that went exactly, but one death stare from Gabby turned his attention, and he handed out the drinks before telling them the next round was on the house.

"Still cute," Brooke said with a sigh as they watched him walk away.

"Still a player," Bella said with an even heavier sigh.

"I think he's just waiting for the right girl to come along," Gabby said. They all looked at her until her cheeks flamed. "What? Don't go saying I read too many romance novels again!"

"I didn't say a word," Jenna said, raising her chin a notch.

The girls were still laughing when Amelia and Maddie appeared with Heidi and Natalie at their side, all eager to catch up and share their news. Maddie was especially proud of her new bakery, and maybe even more excited about her newfound romance if the flush in her cheeks gave anything away. It was like old times, the ten of them together again. Even though Brooke's cousins on either side weren't related to each other, they had all hung out together on holidays as children, and there was no escaping the fact that here in Blue Harbor you knew just about everyone.

Bumped into them too. Brooke's eyes shifted to the bar, where Kyle was now leaning an elbow into the wood, laughing with Jackson.

Her heart began to race, and she swallowed hard as her mind spun. What was Kyle doing here? Shouldn't he be down at Harrison's, working?

Jackson must have called him over. But no, she was flattering herself. Even if Jackson had tipped him off, why would Kyle care enough to stop by? He hadn't cared enough in their short-lived marriage to make concessions for her.

And she was best to remember that, wasn't she?

"I'll grab your drinks," she offered to the cousins who had just arrived.

"You sure?" Amelia asked. Ever the mother hen, Brooke thought, loving that about her cousin. Even as a teen, she was always wise and mature, and a patient listener. She had been one of the few people other than her sisters and parents that Brooke had confided in when she and Kyle had broken up. The rest didn't know the details, or wouldn't understand them. It was perhaps why they couldn't accept that after dating since high school and going through with the wedding, Brooke was ending it.

"Yep," Brooke said firmly, which she covered with what she hoped was a breezy smile.

She took a large sip from her glass and strode to the bar purposefully. Now that she was back in town, she wasn't going to dodge Kyle every chance she had. They'd have to learn to coexist, share space. Something that they hadn't done very well the first time around, had they?

Jackson saw her coming and quickly excused himself to wash some glasses. Kyle took a long pull on his beer and turned, surprise flickering through his gaze when she sauntered up to where he stood.

"Well, this is a surprise," he said.

"The surprise is on me," she said, using his words. "Shouldn't you be down at Harrison's right now?"

It was a sore spot between them, and especially for her, even now, if she were to judge it off the tightness in her chest.

"Ryan's covering things tonight," Kyle said with a shrug.

"I heard he was back," Brooke said, and then, catching the flash in his gaze, felt her cheeks heat. "My family mentioned it last night at dinner."

She didn't know why she should care that he knew they had discussed him. Of course they had discussed him! He was once her husband.

Still was.

"So, he's helping out at the pub, huh?" She could hear the bitter sting to her tone.

He shrugged. "Help might not be the best word."

Brooke resisted the old habit to ask what was going on, to listen, give advice, or just roll her eyes. She knew the history better than anyone, but it wasn't her place anymore. Kyle had made his choice, years ago, to take over the pub and let his brother pursue his career as planned.

He'd made his choice, she reminded herself. And it wasn't to be with her.

Instead of bothering with old wounds, she decided to focus on the future. "I was hoping that we could talk soon."

She eyed him, hoping that he picked up on the urgency of the matter, on the unspoken topic that both of them knew, and only them.

At least, she assumed it was only them. Surely if word got out that she and Kyle had never officially filed for divorce, it would have spread through town faster than a barn fire.

Still, she felt shifty when Jackson reappeared, barely able to suppress his amusement at their expense, and asked if he could get her anything.

"Four glasses of wine for my cousins," she said.

"On the house, as promised." He winked.

Nope. Nothing unusual there. Just Jackson being Jackson. Still, she'd breathe a lot easier once she and Kyle had cleared the air. It was easy to not worry about papers and legalities when she was hundreds of miles away. But being back here, there needed to be rules. And boundaries. And signatures.

A clean break for a fresh start.

Jackson set the glasses on the bar and began pouring.

"What is it you'd like to talk about?" Kyle asked blankly.

Brooke's eyes darted to Jackson, who didn't bother to hide his interest.

She stifled an eye roll. "Now isn't the time. I thought…" Oh, she didn't know what she'd thought! That she could waltz over to him, tell him they needed a divorce, and be done with it?

That would certainly be nice, but she had the sense it wouldn't be so easy.

"I thought that we should talk." She gave him a long look, trying her best to ignore the pull in her gut that came from being this close to him again, from staring into his eyes, the way she had so many other times, back when it filled her with longing, and lust.

She looked away.

He didn't ask what she wanted to discuss, but his neutral expression told her that he probably knew. Maybe he'd been waiting for it.

Maybe, she thought with a squeeze of her stomach, he had been wishing for it.

"I'm usually at Harrison's," he said. "When I'm not home."

She narrowed her eyes on that word. Home. Surely he wasn't implying the little cottage down near the cove with the view of the lake barely visible through the dense trees? How many mornings had she lay on the cool white cotton sheets and looked out over that view?

Not many.

Jackson slid the four glasses of wine to her and disappeared without a word. She struggled to hold them all, happy for the excuse to end this conversation, even if she had initiated it.

"This is a busy week for me. I'm getting my shop off the ground, but I'll find you once I have a chance."

"I'll be here," he said, giving her a long, steady, dare she say suggestive look. "I've always been here."

She blinked at him, unsure what he meant or what he wanted her to say, much less think.

But yes, he had always been here, because he'd chosen to stay behind.

Really, he'd chosen to let her go.

.

4

Brooke was grateful for the work that kept her occupied every waking hour of the following days. She was so busy hanging framed prints, setting up the dressing rooms, which combined totaled close to the entire square footage of her New York City apartment, and selecting which gown she would display in the window for her opening week, that she barely had time to think about Kyle or that fact that he was simply down the street.

The only time she thought of him at all was when she sat down at her newly delivered desk in the corner of the shop, where she could work on a slim white laptop while keeping an eye on the door. The back office was set up with her sewing machine and table, and right off it was the storage room, stacked high with bolts of fabric arranged by color. She had minimal inventory to start with—about twenty gowns in a standard size—as she suspected that the majority of her work would be custom, which suited her just fine. She loved the idea of working closely with a client, hearing their vision, giving them new ideas, and then delivering the wedding dress of their dreams.

Gabby had been helpful, bringing by bunches of white tulips and even tending to the planting in the formerly empty black urns that flanked the front door of the shop. Gus had been installing the sign that day, and Gabby had stood back and admired it with approval.

"Something Blue. I like it!"

"Not very original, but considering we live in Blue Harbor, it made sense." Brooke liked the name, though, and it was one of the reasons that she ultimately chose to go with one of her simple ivory satin gowns in the window—the one that boasted a big blue sash. The dress was so perfect that she decided to leave it simple, with no flowers or confetti or anything else to take attention away. Just a dress to build a dream on.

Brooke sighed, thinking that had she been able to turn back the clock, she might have chosen this dress for her own wedding. Instead, she'd worn something from a catalog, that she'd altered herself, seeing as she was a better seamstress than her mother or sisters. At the time it had been the most beautiful dress she'd ever seen. Perfect really: a sweetheart bodice of lace with a soft tulle skirt that flowed when she walked and moved like a dream.

A dress she had built a dream on. A dream that she had thought Kyle shared.

She righted herself, shaking away the cobwebs of her past, even though they were determined to creep back in, and stick. There was no sense in thinking about that now. Her mind was on other brides. On their special day. She hadn't even considered getting remarried. Technically, she couldn't. Not yet anyway.

She'd waited until her opening day to pull the curtains from the front picture window, letting the sunlight pour through the window, giving the gown the light and airy feeling that it deserved, and bringing the entire room to life. Eventually, she might switch to appointments only, but for now, she needed all the walk-ins she could get.

She almost jumped when the bells over the door chimed within minutes of her turning the sign on the door. She had slipped into the back office, not wanting to stare at a door and wait for it to open, and now she hurried as quickly as she could back to the storefront, trying not to look as nervous as she felt.

A woman with big, blond, curly hair was admiring the dress in the window, and then gasped when she saw the racks of samples that Brooke had worked on in her spare time over the past couple of years. She'd built up quite a collection. Enough to make the room feel filled but still spacious. Enough to demonstrate her range, but clearly define her style, which was classic, but fresh, or at least that's what she liked to think.

Her boss back in New York had thought otherwise. Thought that Brooke was trying too hard. That she should stick with what she knew. In other words, tried and true, boring designs, for everyday wear. Nothing that excited Brooke or challenged her creative spirit. And even then, she'd managed to come up short.

"Can I help you?" Brooke asked, careful to give the client space to browse. She remembered when the store was a women's clothing shop that Patsy would pounce on customers as soon as they walked in the door, often following them around the room as they considered blouses, sweaters, and dresses. She was never shy with her opinion, either.

"I have been eagerly waiting for this store to open since the moment I heard about it!" The woman flashed her a big smile, and Brooke relaxed.

"When is your big day?" she asked the woman.

"Late July." The woman gave her another smile. "After the Cherry Festival, mind you, because there is no way that I'm going to miss that event, even for my honeymoon. You'll be invited, of course."

Brooke blinked as it all clicked. This was Candy! Of course, she would be the first one in her shop if she was as eager as her cousins claimed her to be. Still, Brooke couldn't help but feel a little deflated that the first customer was someone she was going to be related to, meaning the visit fell under family support.

"You're marrying my Uncle Dennis!" She was everything that Britt and her sisters had claimed her to be. And more.

Candy thrust out her hand so that Brooke could admire the diamond engagement ring. She was slightly taken aback, only to realize that this was probably something she should get used to. Her customers would be engaged, eager to share their happiness. It was the most blissful period of their life.

At least, it had been for her. After that, well, reality set in. And fast.

"It's beautiful," she said, admiring the stone. She couldn't help but also notice Candy's bright pink painted nails, which also matched the polish on her toes peeking out of her open-toed shoes. She didn't need to ask what color theme Candy had chosen for her big day. It was fairly obvious. Still, she wanted to make conversation. And get to know her new aunt.

"Do you have much planned?"

Candy's eyes burst open and she rolled back her head, laughing so loudly and with such unabashed energy that Brooke couldn't help but join in, even though she suspected she was the brunt of the joke.

"Oh, honey, I have an entire binder busting open with ideas. I've only been planning my wedding since I was ten!"

First marriage then. Even though it wasn't Dennis's, Brooke felt it was safe to assume that Candy would want the biggest, whitest dress she could find. With a veil and a train. And a garter.

Possibly, she'd try to get Uncle Dennis to play that little game where he removed it with his teeth while everyone stood in a circle, watching. Brooke could only hope that there would be an open bar.

Candy pulled her tote from her shoulder and fished out a large binder. She hadn't been joking or exaggerating. Brooke blinked in surprise at the heft of the thing.

"That's impressive!" She could immediately tell that if Candy was organized like her, they would get along fine. Brooke couldn't go anywhere without her planner these days. She loved nothing more than sitting down to it each night and outlining her following day. It eased her mind. Calmed her.

Some might say it gave her a false sense of security.

"Oh, this is nothing. This binder here is just for my dress ideas," Candy said. "You should see my floral binder. I'm going over to see Gabby if I have time before I'm needed back at the café."

Brooke could only assume that she would be hearing about it from her sister, and soon.

"Amelia mentioned that you work for her." Brooke left off the part that Amelia had also mentioned on Saturday night that she sometimes needed to send Candy on long errands, just to get a moment's peace. No doubt Candy's wedding planning was coming in handy lately.

Sure enough, Candy beamed. "And she has been so generous when it comes to me needing time for this wedding!"

"I can see you've thought it all out." Brooke eyed the binder, wondered what could be in there.

"I must have a thousand ideas," Candy said gaily. "I want it to be perfect."

Brooke felt her smile slip. Perfect set the bar high—both for a dress and a marriage.

She swallowed hard, and said a little weakly, "Well, we could sit down and you can show me? Or maybe if you look around, something will jump out at you?"

Candy walked over to the sitting area that Brooke had set up and dropped her binder onto the white marble coffee table with a *thud*. The thing weighed so much that Brooke took a subtle peek to make sure no damage had been made to her new purchase. Instead of sitting down on one of the blush-colored velvet chairs that Brooke had ordered for the shop, Candy scurried over to another rack of dresses.

"Oh, it's so hard to choose! They're all so wonderful. Everyone in your family told me how talented you were, but this has exceeded my expectations!"

Brooke felt her cheeks flush at the compliment, which she took as sincere, even if Candy was technically family. Almost.

"It's been a life's dream, honestly," she admitted. Not the wedding dress part, technically, that had come later. But being in full control of her creativity had always been the dream.

Being back in Blue Harbor had not, she thought, inhaling a sigh. But as she'd learned over the years, nothing ever went completely as planned.

"You don't miss New York?" Candy asked as she absentmindedly sifted through a rack of dresses.

Brooke considered that for a moment. Once, she couldn't get to New York fast enough. Once, that had been her life's dream, to live in the big city, to be a part of the fashion industry, to be right in the pack, at the center of the action.

It was all she'd wanted. More than anything.

More, she thought looking back, than Kyle.

She swallowed against the guilt that always weighed heavy in her chest when she thought back on that time in her life.

"New York was where I needed to be for my twenties," Brooke said matter-of-factly. "But I accomplished everything I wanted. I traveled. I worked for a major designer."

"And then you got fired?" Candy winced dramatically and bit her lip. "Sorry, hon. Your mother told me."

Brooke shrugged it off. No sense in getting defensive over the facts, even if it did sting. She'd be lying if she said her ego hadn't been bruised until Gabby had given her a pep talk over the phone and insisted that this was a blessing in disguise, that it wasn't that she wasn't good enough. It was that she was *too* good.

She smiled now thinking of her sister. That kind of support made coming back here worth everything. Even seeing Kyle.

"It's okay. It wasn't my dream job after all. I always wanted to bring my visions to life. And if I can do that while being around my family, all the better."

"Family." Candy held out her arms and wiggled her fingers. "Can I? Sorry, I'm a hugger."

Brooke bit her lip to keep from laughing. This woman couldn't be more different than her Aunt Elizabeth had been, but she was warm and open and welcoming. And she was a customer. She was everything that Brooke needed right now.

She shrugged her agreement and let Candy pull her in for a long, squishy hug, which Brooke had to admit did feel good. Since returning to Blue Harbor, she'd been hugged at least a dozen times, which was probably more than she'd been hugged in all of her years in New York, where the double air kiss was more standard.

"Family!" Candy said, pulling back and giving her a long look. "My, you're just as pretty as your sisters!"

Brooke blushed again. Everyone knew that Gabby was the real beauty in the family. And still single. What did that say for her own chance of finding love again?

She halted that thought immediately. Honestly, it was the opening day of her shop! She had a willing customer standing before her. And she was technically still a married woman! She absolutely could not even entertain the thought of dating again. It was the dresses, and Candy's excitement. It was hard not to get swept away.

That had been by design. It wasn't supposed to be a trap.

Quickly, she turned her focus back to Candy. "Let's take a few moments to look through your binder. Can I get you a tea or coffee?"

"Tea, please," Candy said with a light in her eye. "Extra sugar. In case my name doesn't already give you a hint, I like things sweet."

*

By the time Candy left the shop, Brooke was exhausted and her hand was cramped from writing down so many ideas. There had been no further patrons, not that she had expected a flood of customers, though that would have been nice. Still, she had one firm client and some design ideas to sketch that would keep her busy for the remainder of the afternoon. Seeing as it was already lunchtime, she saw no reason not to take a short break and stretch her legs.

Normally she might have popped by Sweet Stems to see if Gabby wanted to grab something from the café, but knowing that Candy was headed that way was enough to make her rethink her plans.

And get the conversation with Kyle over with, she thought, as her stomach turned with dread.

She turned the sign on her door, locked it behind her, and walked down Main Street in her heels and shift dress, feeling more the young, naïve girl who had marched down the aisle to take Kyle's hand rather than the confident, successful businesswoman that the reflection in the store windows claimed her to be. She could dress any part, but feeling it was a very different thing, and right now, she felt nearly as out of place in her hometown as she had her first few months in New York.

With any luck, Kyle would only see her outward appearance, not her innermost feelings.

Really, she probably didn't need any luck at all. A request for a divorce, after nearly six years apart and no contact during that entire time, was long overdue. Surely he was just as eager as she was to end things once and for all.

Harrison's was down at the next block and across the street, and Brooke hurried her pace so she wouldn't lose her nerve. But as she approached the weathered wood door with the rusty, oversized handle, she hesitated, only before reminding herself that this had to be done. For her business. For herself.

Stick to the plan, she scolded herself firmly, even if yet again, Kyle had the power to complicate things. Kyle may not have wanted to support her dream all those years ago, but she wasn't going to let him stop her now.

With that, she flung open the door and blinked against the change of light. Harrison's had always been dark inside, with the blinds pulled tight most weeks of the year, but still, it was an adjustment from the sunny day outside.

She scanned the room, not surprised to find that it hadn't changed at all, just as her sisters had said. That it was the same nautical-themed bar that it had always been, since before Kyle took over. It was a time warp. Or a landmark, as some might say.

But to her, it was her nemesis. It was because of this pub, and Kyle's insistence on holding onto the past, that they hadn't been able to look to the future together.

Behind the bar, she spotted him, his back to her, his arms folded across his chest, deep in what appeared to be a tense discussion with Ryan of all people. Ryan, the best man at their wedding, of course, Ryan who had already spotted her and was now giving an exaggerated look of shock, clutching his chest as his eyes gleamed.

Had Kyle not mentioned she was back? She felt a flicker of something far too close to disappointment. Why should she care that Kyle didn't bother to mention this to his brother? There was no reason for Kyle to talk about her, right?

The grin on Ryan's face caused Kyle to turn and look distractedly over his shoulder. His frown lifted for a hint of a second, so quickly that it wasn't entirely noticeable, but she noticed. She knew him so well.

"Well, well. Brooke Conway. Is that really you?" Ryan's voice boomed loud enough for a few of the guys at the table near the window to shift their eyes from the television screen for a moment. "I almost didn't notice you in that fancy outfit."

Brooke looked down at her navy linen sheath dress and heeled sandals. "I'm simply dressed for work. I own a boutique down the street."

"You don't say!" Ryan's look was accusatory when it fell on Kyle, who ignored it. "What kind of boutique?"

Brooke lifted her chin a notch and braced herself for it. "I'm a wedding dress designer."

There was a split-second pause where she wasn't sure if Ryan might laugh. "A wedding dress designer. Well. Isn't that…"

"Wonderful," Kyle cut in, shooting his brother a dirty look. He shifted his gaze back to Brooke, locking it there. "It's really wonderful."

Brooke stared back at him, overwhelmed with sudden emotion at the tenderness in his eyes and the sincerity in his tone, her heart weighing heavy with the creeping sense of guilt and confusion that always happened when she thought about Kyle. Now, standing in front of him, it was impossible not to see the same kind blue eyes that had looked so deeply into hers when he'd gotten down on one knee, and later, when he'd stood at the altar, watching her walk down the aisle, and then, took her hand.

She closed her eyes against the memory, against his gaze. When she opened them, he turned away, busied himself drying glasses.

"You have a few minutes to talk?" She darted a look at Ryan, who seemed to show no intention of leaving.

Kyle jutted his chin at his brother. "Take ten."

Ryan slid another glance at Brooke before he left. A warning glance, if she didn't know better.

"Sorry about him," Kyle said, once Ryan had disappeared into the kitchen.

She gave a small smile, finding strange comfort in being alone with him. "I can come back later if this is a bad time."

"It's fine," Kyle said. He held up a bottle of chilled white wine—Conway brand, her name across the label per the family tradition that her father and Dennis had set in place years back, naming each new blend after one of their daughters.

She was touched that he would stock her namesake wine. Confused, too. But she wouldn't read into it. Most restaurants and bars in town stocked Conway wine, of course. People in Blue Harbor liked to support each other.

She hoped that extended to Kyle.

"Can I offer you something?"

She shook her head, refusing the drink, even though she could really use something to calm her pounding heart and take away her nerves right now. Was it so strange to be asking for a divorce, now, after all this time?

It was. Because for whatever reason, and one she couldn't even explain to herself, she hadn't asked for one earlier.

And neither had he.

There was no reason to hesitate, she knew. She had the loan to think about. Her long list of items to scratch off her business plan if she ever intended to grow it and make a success. She'd never get it approved if her credit was still tied to this pub, for starters. And nothing was keeping her connected to Kyle anymore but a piece of paper. What was another piece of paper at this point?

"I have to get back to work soon, so, I'm good."

He set down the wine with a shrug. "Maybe another time."

She narrowed her gaze. Nope, not reading into that either. Besides, maybe it was good that he was keeping things so friendly. It showed that there were no hard feelings.

"So...a wedding dress shop?" He cocked an eyebrow.

"Does that surprise you?" she asked, noticing the defensive edge creeping into her tone. She braced herself for it, knowing that it would come.

"I seem to remember a girl who didn't want to design clothing for commercial gain, but for the art."

Maybe he was teasing her, but she'd learned over the years that there was a hint of truth in every joke, and Kyle was speaking the cold hard facts. She had taken on a job as a designer for a major brand, where her creativity was stifled, and the only gain was in the form of a paycheck that paid the rent each month with a little left over on the side for her new dream.

Because thanks to Kyle, she'd had to shift the idea of her future. Make it one without him in it.

"And I remember a guy who wanted to design custom furniture," she replied, immediately regretting her words when she saw the way he pulled back, all hint of amusement now gone from his face. She softened her tone. "Do you still make furniture?"

"Who has the time?" He shrugged, evading her eyes. "I'm a bar owner now."

Brooke closed her mouth, feeling a wave of disappointment that she had no claim to. Kyle had been a skilled carpenter. He was creative and passionate and detail-oriented. He'd dreamed of opening a showroom, making one-of-a-kind pieces with his two hands and his whole heart.

But that had been his dream, not hers. Even if she'd shared it. Once.

He set both hands on the bar and leaned forward. "I get the impression there's something you need to say."

She resisted the urge to take a step back, to put physical distance between herself and Kyle. It had worked so well all this time. Eventually, those deep-set eyes and that crooked smile had faded from her mind. But now, he was right in front of her. And damn it if he wasn't making all of this much more difficult than it should be.

"I'm going to be applying for a business loan soon," she explained, even though there was no reason to bother with personal details. "And, well, I think it's time that we make our relationship status official."

There was a beat of silence. "You want a divorce?"

She glanced around, but none of the day drinkers were listening and the television was loud.

"I think it's time," she said simply. When he didn't respond right away, she added, "Don't you?"

Kyle pulled in a breath and stepped back from the bar. "And here I thought you might want to catch up."

She froze for a second, until she saw his mouth quirk into a smile. "It's been a long time, Kyle," she said softly.

His eyes lingered on her. "It has been, Bee."

Bee. That had been his nickname for her, all those years ago, and not just because it was the initial of her first name. She'd loved bumblebees, even as a kid when her sisters would run from them, squealing. He used to tell her that was a trait that he'd admired in her. That she wasn't scared. That she didn't let a little insect stop her from picking a flower she wanted.

That she didn't let anything stand in her way.

Could he say the same now, after what happened between them?

She knew she couldn't.

*

Kyle knew he shouldn't be surprised. Brooke wanted a divorce. Considering it had been almost six years since she'd packed her bags and left the home they'd shared, and then, days later, Blue Harbor, he knew he shouldn't be surprised. Eventually, he might have asked for one too, assumed he would, that he'd have to ask Gabby or Jenna for her contact information, track her down. He assumed someday he'd move on with his life. When the time came, he'd deal with it.

He just hadn't expected that time to be now. Because he hadn't moved on, but rather stayed in one place, doing the same thing, day after day, not thinking about the future. And seeing Brooke again only stirred up everything they'd once had, rather than what they'd lost.

From the pinch of her mouth, he assumed that she didn't feel the same way.

She cleared her throat and looked away. "I need to get back to my shop soon."

He didn't try to disguise his disappointment. "So you've filed then?"

"Not yet," she said slowly. "I thought it was better to speak to you first. We owe it to each other."

His heart began to pick up speed, and he did his best to keep his expression relaxed. Her face was impossible to read, but two things were certain: she wanted a divorce. And she hadn't sought one out before today. He didn't want to push things by asking why she had waited so long when he didn't have a good answer himself. He chose instead to focus on the information at hand, and where that left him. Where that left *them*.

"How soon do you want to apply for this loan?" he asked, keeping his voice conversational.

She looked surprised at the question. "Soon," she said, licking her bottom lip. She was nervous. She'd had that tick for as long as he'd known her, which was basically his entire life.

He nodded, considering his options. He hadn't thought about Brooke in a while, not properly at least. At first, she was all he thought about, but the pub soon consumed his waking hours, and he'd learned to get through the days on his own. In the back of his mind, he knew that she was always out there, sure. That she was his wife, in the legal sense of the word.

But seeing her now, separated by only a two-foot-wide bar of polished wood, all he could think of was that she *was* his wife. His sweet, creative, beautiful wife. The woman who made him laugh. The woman who had made him love. And he wasn't ready to let that go so easily the second time around.

The blond hair that once splayed on the pillow beside him was close enough to reach out and stroke; the blue eyes that would crinkle when she smiled now stared at him with a strange detachment.

"It will take a while for the paperwork to process, but...I don't want anything."

Old hurts stirred up. "No, you never did."

Brooke sucked in a breath and released it slowly. She lowered her eyes. She waited.

Finally, Kyle said the only reasonable thing there was to say. "I'll sign. I'll make it straightforward."

She nodded, her gaze still fixated on her hands, which were resting on the bar. Her rings were gone, of course. He'd kept them in his bedside drawer, ever since she'd left them on the dresser that last morning they were together.

"On one condition," he said, seeing his chance. His last one, by the looks of it.

Her eyes shot up to him warily. "What condition?"

He hesitated, wondering if he could really go through with it. He had nothing to lose…but everything.

"We spend a little time together first."

"A little time together?" She pursed her lips together and sighed. "Kyle, what's done is done. Why make this any more difficult than it needs to be?"

Interesting, he thought, narrowing his eyes on her. Or maybe, that was wishful thinking. But if there was a chance in hell that Brooke still had any feelings left for him, now was the time to find out.

He'd let her slip away once before. He'd be damned if he let it happen twice.

5

Brooke boiled the entire walk back to the shop, pounding the pavement so hard, she was surprised she hadn't broken a heel on her designer (albeit sample sale) shoes.

Spend time together? What was Kyle thinking? They hadn't spent time together in almost six years, and the last few days of their relationship were nothing to hold on to—if anything, they were something to forget.

They'd been arguing. A lot. Brooke had been given the opportunity of a lifetime—a job for a well-known designer, in New York City. It was an entry-level position, but it sure beat the women's boutique on Main Street. It was her chance.

It was supposed to be *their* chance. That had been the plan, hadn't it? They'd go to New York or Los Angeles or even Chicago—together. Two creative minds determined to make their mark. It wouldn't be easy, but it was exciting. He'd get a day job while he built up a following for his furniture, shopping his designs at trendy boutiques. They'd go to gallery openings and charity events to network; they'd host dinner parties right on the hand-carved table that Kyle had honed as a wedding gift to her. They'd be a partnership. A team.

Only when the time came to go, Kyle changed course.

They'd fought. They'd argued. Neither one of them had backed down.

Brooke had eventually left. And Kyle didn't come after her.

She'd waited. Kept the phone on, checked for messages even when her screen was blank. She'd resisted the urge to call, knowing that she'd only be repeating what she'd already said. That this was her dream. His dream. Their dream. That they were married. That they were supposed to be starting a life together.

That he wasn't supposed to lock himself into a life in Blue Harbor out of guilt or obligation. That she didn't want this for him.

That his father wouldn't have, either.

But those were words she'd held back, knowing that they'd cut too deep, too soon after his father's fatal heart attack.

Kyle was doing what he needed to do. And she, she was doing what she needed to do. Eventually, she stopped checking her phone. Stopped hoping for a message. Stopped believing that he would come to his senses, or miss her.

And eventually, she'd moved on with her new life, alone.

No, Brooke thought, as she finished out her first day at the shop, one eye on the window and the other on her spreadsheets, where she was business planning four seasons out, putting her into next spring. No, there was nothing good that could come from spending time with Kyle.

Well, other than getting him to agree to a quick and straightforward divorce.

*

By Friday afternoon, Brooke was almost hoping to see Kyle, if only to get things finished once and for all. If he didn't stop by soon, she'd have to hunt him down, repeat her request, or take matters into her own hands and consult an attorney to draw up the paperwork on her terms. It was an option, but it wasn't the one she wanted to take. She didn't want to engage in petty arguments or try to get a cut of anything. She just wanted to make their lives officially separate. To do what she'd been doing for six years for the rest of her life. Build her career. Focus on her routine.

Make a plan she could stick to and count on.

She sucked in a breath as a customer swept out of the dressing room, her eyes shining and her smile radiant as she admired herself in the three-way gilded mirror. It was one of Brooke's newer designs, one she had created with spring on the mind, in an off-white lace with spaghetti straps and an A-line skirt. The bodice was her favorite part of the dress, with a dramatic deep V-neck cut that highlighted the collarbone. It fit the customer perfectly.

"Spring brides are the prettiest brides," the bride's mother clucked from the corner.

Brooke opened her mouth to chime in that she had once been a late spring bride too, but fortunately she realized her error before she had a chance to dampen what was turning out to be a very pleasant ending to her work week.

"This dress fits you as if it were custom made for you," Brooke said. "How do you feel in it?"

The bride sucked in a breath and blew it out slowly. In the mirror, she met Brooke's eye. "Like it was made for me. It's the one!"

Brooke managed not to show her excitement—or her surprise—by smiling serenely and saying, "Perfect."

Because it was perfect. Not just the dress, but the fact that she had managed to sell one of her off-the-rack gowns in her opening week, and she had commissioned two others—Candy's, and a lovely childhood friend of Jenna's who wasn't getting married until next winter, leaving Brooke with plenty of time to come up with some cold-weather concepts.

She moved back to her desk quickly to write up the invoice while the bride changed out of the gown.

"We'll keep the dress here in the back room until your big day," she explained. "And of course we'll schedule your fittings closer to the date. Do you live in the area? I feel like I should know everyone, but then, I've been away for a while."

The bride shook her head. "Pine Falls."

The next town over. Brooke was quietly pleased to see that she was already drawing business beyond the border of Blue Harbor. With any luck, word would soon spread.

"Do you have anything for bridesmaids?" the bride asked hopefully.

Brooke hesitated. She didn't want to spread herself too thin from the onset, but expanding to bridesmaid dresses was part of her long-term plan.

"By special order," she said, seeing an opportunity to add some extra pages to her lookbook which sat on the marble coffee table for brides to flip through in their design meetings. She felt a little shaky going off-plan like this, but she also knew that this type of request could push her out of her comfort zone and help her to achieve her goals sooner.

"I have a few ideas in mind. Could I stop by next week and show you some magazine clippings?"

Brooke set up the appointment in her calendar, accepted the deposit for the dress, and managed not to do a little victory dance until the door was closed behind the blushing bride and her proud mother.

She only managed to stop once she heard the jingling of the door opening behind her, and she turned to see Kyle grinning back at her. From the gleam in his eyes, there was no doubt he'd witnessed that little performance. She supposed she should be thankful that it wasn't a potential customer, but she couldn't fight the flush from heating her cheeks.

"Practicing your dance moves?" he asked, his tone laced with amusement.

"Very funny," she said drolly. Still, she wasn't going to let Kyle ruin her good mood, even if she was a little curious, and worried, about his motive for being here, whereas her motives had been laid out, crystal clear.

"Actually," she said, "I was celebrating. I sold a dress off the rack today, and I was also asked to come up with some designs for the bridesmaids."

Kyle looked dutifully impressed. "This calls for a celebration."

It did. But not with him. She'd toast with a good crisp glass of wine one night this weekend with one of her sisters or cousins. In other words, people who had supported her dreams, and stuck around long enough to see them through.

"Suddenly eager to support me?" There was an edge to her tone that betrayed her inner hurt, but she couldn't deny it.

Kyle frowned at her. "I always supported you, Brooke."

She resisted the urge to laugh out loud, not that what he'd said was funny. "That's not the way I remember it, but then, I guess none of that matters now. I'm happy where I've landed."

He raised an eyebrow. "Right back in Blue Harbor, you mean? The very town you just had to leave to make something of yourself?"

She pressed her lips together. There was so much she could say, but it wouldn't help matters, or change anything. Instead, she stuck to the facts. "I wouldn't be where I am now if I hadn't been given the experiences I had in New York."

She lifted her chin a notch higher, seeing the squint of his gaze that told her he didn't believe her, not completely at least. This was what happened when someone knew you as well as Kyle knew her.

Or had known her. Once.

After all, she'd changed. And not only in the way that she dressed. She had gone from a sheltered home life in a small town to a marriage to her childhood sweetheart to living alone and making something of herself in a huge, strange city. She'd learned more than the street names and the neighborhoods. She'd learned to be alone, to speak up for herself, to fight for what she wanted.

Which was why she wasn't going to let this man get under her skin. She wanted something from him, and she was going to do what it took to make that happen.

Even if he was determined to make it quite difficult, to say the least.

"And you just decided to walk away from that fabulous job?" Kyle peered at her. "I mean, it was your dream job, at least that's how you described it when you left."

She sniffed. "People grow out of positions," she explained. She picked up a stack of paperwork and straightened the pages.

His eyes narrowed. "Unless…"

She firmed her lips together and willed herself not to lose her temper. "I was fired. Happy? It seems that I was too determined to come up with new ideas than keep my eyes on my desk and do what I was told."

He actually laughed, but she didn't take offense. "You always were ambitious."

"We both were," she replied, giving him a pointed look as she set the papers into a crisp, labeled folder.

His expression immediately sobered. He stuffed his hands into his pockets as he took in his surroundings, jutting his bottom lip as he nodded. "Well, this is quite a shop. I haven't been in here in a long time, but I can see what you've done to the place. It's very...pretty."

She could tell by his struggle to form his opinion that he wasn't saying what he really meant. That this was not what she'd once said she wanted. That she had spent enough time within these very four walls to need to escape them above all else.

Above him.

"Thank you," she said, suppressing a sigh. What she wanted to ask was why he was here, but she had a feeling they would get to that before he left if they weren't interrupted first.

She glanced out the window, hoping that a passerby might save her from standing here, alone, with Kyle. Was it always this quiet in the shop? She made a mental note to turn the volume on the stereo system a notch higher. The classical music was fine for her clientele, but it did nothing to relieve the tension that was building in her as Kyle sauntered around the room, giving it his full attention.

"You pulled this together quickly," he noted.

She was happy that he had paused at the end of the room. With any luck, he would stay there. The more physical distance there was between them, the better, she'd come to realize.

She shrugged. "Patsy was accommodating given our history. She had the walls patched and repainted when she cleared out. All I had to do was get some lights installed and order a bit of furniture."

"You really made all of these?" He looked baffled as he reached for a particularly frothy triple-layer tulle gown. Brooke twitched. She had to all but force herself not to make everyone wash their hands as they entered the boutique.

"I did." She quickly walked to where he stood and gently moved the dress back into its place. "And no two are alike." A quick inspection revealed no smudges. White was such an unforgiving color. Still, she'd probably make friends with the current owners of the dry cleaner in town.

"Like snowflakes then?" He grinned, and despite herself, she felt her heart soften to him, to the kindness in his eyes, to the ease of his conversation. She remembered now, something she had so easily forgotten. How whenever they would walk in the snow, she would open her mitten and study the design of each tiny flake until they melted, never to be replaced.

When had she stopped doing that? Stopping to admire nature, beauty in its simplest form?

Around the time she'd left Blue Harbor. Around the time she'd hardened her heart.

She looked away quickly and smoothed the skirt of the dress. "I think my customers want to feel unique. Even if they buy something off the rack instead of opting for a custom design, they'll know it's still special, just for them. A special dress for a special day."

Shoot. She regretted the words the moment they slipped out, and the heavy silence in the room only heightened her misstep. She swallowed hard, averting her gaze, but it wasn't possible to ignore Kyle forever. Not when they lived in the same town. Not when he was standing in her shop. So close that she could reach out and touch him if she wanted to.

"Our day was pretty special," Kyle said. "At least I'd like to think so."

Brooke didn't reply. She'd tried hard not to think of that day. Of the butterflies in her stomach when she'd taken her father's arm, of the sight of her sisters walking in front of her, in their navy dresses, clutching apricot bouquets.

"Well, I can see that you put a lot of hard work into this," Kyle finally said, and Brooke breathed in relief, giving him a grateful smile.

"I did. It's something I've been working toward for a long time."

"Wedding dresses?" Again, he didn't look convinced.

"I always liked high fashion," she reminded him. "And...and I wasn't able to be as creative as I had hoped in my day job in New York."

"I know that feeling," he said dryly.

She sensed a shift in tone, perhaps an opening to talk about his life, and she nearly took the bait. But no, Kyle had made his decision, and she'd come to accept that.

Even if it seemed now that he might not be as happy with the outcome as she was.

"Can I help you with something?" she asked, straightening her shoulders and tidying an already tidy rack of gowns. She glanced at the clock on the far wall. It was closing in on the end of the day, meaning the chances of someone stopping in now were very slim.

"I'm following up on our conversation from the other day."

Her heart skipped a beat. She kept her expression neutral and focused on the gowns, forcing a steadying breath before replying. "And?"

She looked at him, hating the way her body betrayed her head. So the man was attractive. He was also all wrong for her. Always had been. She just hadn't seen that soon enough.

"And I'm here to ask if you're free?"

Free? She gaped at him, her heart beginning to pound. So he hadn't come to his senses, hadn't realized that there was no point in spending time together when their relationship had ended nearly six years ago.

And he hadn't just been having fun with her either. No, everything about him, from the look in his eyes to his presence in her shop meant that he was sincere. And she wasn't so sure that she wanted to know why.

"I don't see a point to this," she said wearily. "If you wanted to talk sooner, you could have found me."

He didn't argue with her. Didn't explain himself either. "Harborside Creamery. I seem to recall you never could resist their raspberry ice cream. What do you say?"

It was true that she did like the raspberry ice cream at Harborside and that she had searched all of Manhattan for a shop to rival it, and had come out of that experience disappointed and probably five pounds heavier.

Ice cream wasn't dinner or even drinks. And if it would get Kyle to sign on the dotted line, then she supposed it was worth it.

"One ice cream and then you'll sign the papers?"

"That's pretty quick, don't you think?"

She stared at him. "Six years is hardly impulsive, Kyle."

"What about…six dates." Perhaps catching the widening of her eyes, he said, "Meet-ups. Whatever you want to call them."

She shook her head, unable to hold back her curiosity any longer. "Why, Kyle? To punish me? To hold me back from moving on with my life? Are you still mad?"

It was a foolish question. After all, she was still mad at him. Madder now that he was putting her through this…game. Test. Whatever it was.

His expression softened long enough to make her shoulders relax. "We haven't seen each other in nearly six years, Brooke."

"One date for each year, then?" She didn't know whether to laugh or cry. Cry, she realized, noticing that her hands had started to shake. It was bad enough standing here, alone with him. How was she supposed to get through six dates with him? Because that's what they were. She knew it. He knew it.

"It's like you said. We owe it to each other. Sure, we parted ways—"

"We ended things," she corrected him.

His eyes seemed to frown. "We have a lot of shared memories, Brooke. A lot of history. Don't you think we owe it to each other, just to be sure? Besides, we've waited this long. What are six more dates?" He looked at her plainly, and she realized that he wasn't going to change his mind.

And he wasn't going to change hers either, she thought firmly. If that was what he intended to do.

"Fine. Six *meet-ups*. But I can't drag this out, Kyle. I have a business to run, and a loan to apply for if I'm going to grow the way I want to and—"

He was smiling now, but it no longer met his eyes. "Just six. I'll see you at Harborside Creamery. Tonight. Say…seven?"

He wasn't leaving her a choice. And she was all out of words for him. With a nod, she turned and went into her small office, only releasing her breath when she sank back against the closed door.

Six dates with her husband was a small price to pay to move on with her life once and for all. She picked up a pen and drew six lines in the bottom corner of her planner and then flipped back to her business plan, trying to keep her mind on the future, even if her heart was suddenly being pulled back into the past.

6

An ice cream date didn't call for much preparation, Brooke decided as she studied the offerings of her closet. And really, this wasn't a date at all. It was a meeting. Or a *meet-up*.

It was blackmail, that's what it was.

Still, there was no reason to show up in her sweats and a threadbare cotton tee, which was what she usually changed into at the end of a long day of work. It was a warm spring night, and so Brooke put on her favorite jeans that barely skimmed her ankles, a simple white scoop-neck tee, and grabbed a blush pink wrap sweater in case the breeze off the lake picked up.

Not that she'd be out for long. She could finish that ice cream in two and a half minutes if need be—she and her sisters used to have various ice cream eating contests as kids. Who could eat the slowest on a cooler day, and who could eat the fastest on those hot, muggy evenings in August when their treats started to melt and trickle down their hands, leaving them sticky.

She held the prize for fastest ice cream eater, even if she did get a brain freeze. Knowing this, she felt better. She'd be in and out and home in her sweats in about fifteen minutes, factoring in the walk to and from the parlor.

Or maybe she'd stop by the Carriage House Inn afterward, see if anyone she knew was in the pub so she could toast to the success of her opening week with a glass of champagne.

She started to laugh as she reached for her keys in the bowl near the back door of her apartment. Who was she kidding? This was Blue Harbor and it was a Friday night. Of course, she would bump into someone she knew tonight. Even at the creamery.

And how would that go exactly? If one of her sisters or cousins or even one of her old friends that she was yet to catch up with saw her sharing a table with her so-called ex, there would be a lot of explaining to do.

She tried to look on the bright side. Maybe it would be better to run into family or friends than to sit alone with Kyle, a man whom she hadn't shared even ice cream with since she was still carefree and young and full of hope and promise. Maybe bumping into someone wouldn't lead to explanation, but rather, distraction that would spare her more awkward conversation with Kyle. Maybe Kyle would realize after tonight there was no sense in dragging out the inevitable. That there was nothing left to talk about, even after all these years apart. They'd catch up, summarize the past six years, and then be left with nothing else to say.

Yes, that would be her mission. Kyle might think he had gotten his way by getting her to agree to this ridiculous ice cream date, but she planned to use her time wisely, and she'd be spending it convincing him that the only thing they owed each other was to officially go their separate ways.

*

Kyle tapped on the half-closed door to the back office and poked his head around to see his brother crouched over an ancient computer screen. Normally he'd crack a joke in this situation, tell Ryan that this wasn't an office job, even if it was hard to find humor in the situation. The pub was barely covering the bills, and already staffing was lean. Some months he didn't take home a paycheck, not that he was complaining. Feeling sorry for himself was something he'd never done, not when his dad had died, not when he'd given up his dreams of having his own furniture line to take over this place.

Not even when Brooke had left.

"You got the bar covered tonight?"

Pouring drinks wasn't Ryan's specialty, but luckily, none of the patrons of the pub asked for anything too complicated. No strange cocktails with funny names, nope. This was a beer and whiskey type of place, maybe the occasional glass of wine and usually only when a lady showed up, which was rare.

It wasn't how he would have wanted it to be, but he respected it all the same. This pub wasn't just an institution, it was the last remaining part of their father he still had. His old man had taken pride in it, made it what he wanted it to be, and who was Kyle to undo those efforts?

He knew Ryan had a point. He wasn't oblivious to the dark blinds, the scuffed floors, the limited menu, or the general vibe of the place, which was not exactly modern and not somewhere you'd take a date, not that he was dating much. It was a place to grab some drinks, watch the game, throw some darts, and not care if you were wearing your fishing clothes, either. His father didn't care about pretense. He cared about community. About welcoming everyone, not putting on airs. Good drinks, good food, good company. That was his motto, and it was one that Kyle had upheld.

Competition was stiff for a small town: tourism made sure of that. There were the dockside bars and the gastropubs and the nautical-themed places along the lakefront to contend with. Harrison's had always prided itself on being a locals' joint, but more and more locals preferred the Carriage House Inn, something he had tried to deny over the past few years.

"Staring at those numbers all day won't make them change," he said, only half-joking. He could easily be accused of doing the same thing now and again.

They were running on fumes, and if they stood a chance at making it another fifty years—heck, five years—then they'd need a loan. And they'd need to qualify for one.

He hadn't taken over his father's legacy only to put it out of business. Hadn't given up the last six years of his life to end up shutting the doors.

Hadn't given up Brooke to end up with not just an empty home but also an empty pub.

"I suppose it's enough for one day." Ryan sighed and pushed back his chair. His visible fatigue turned to a look of familiar brotherly banter when he grinned. "You got a hot date or something?"

He made a grand gesture of looking Kyle up and down, drawing attention to the fact that instead of his faded jeans and soft cotton tee-shirt, Kyle was wearing a polo and khaki shorts.

Kyle shook his head, brushing him off. Growing up, they'd always teased, and he hadn't minded it so much back then. Something had changed when Ryan went away to college and Kyle stayed behind, finishing high school and then going to a local college, not aspiring to the nine-to-five corporate gig that Ryan had pursued. Kyle had worked at the pub to get by and save up, and he knew that Ryan thought he was better somehow.

Kyle had ignored it. He was doing what he loved. He was marrying the girl he loved. And his future—it was all mapped out.

He didn't like thinking back on that time in his life. On the impossible choices he'd made. On the loss he'd felt over his father, and then, soon after, over Brooke.

"Just heading out," he said tightly.

"Heading out with the hopes of seeing a certain ex-wife?" Ryan raised an eyebrow.

"Nope, not planning to run into an ex-wife tonight," Kyle said honestly. Everyone had assumed when Brooke left town and never returned that they'd officially ended things. For all appearances, their marriage was over. He never talked about Brooke. He even dated a bit, here and there, nothing serious. He told himself that she wasn't coming back. That if she'd planned to, she would have returned by now, that she'd given up. Didn't want contact. Didn't even want to deal with speaking to him enough to get a divorce. When she visited, she didn't look him up, and he only found out about it after she'd left. He tried not to keep count. Tried not to think of her at all.

But now, well, now all that reason was replaced with something a heck of a lot more confusing.

"You gone for the night then?" Ryan was no doubt concerned about handling a full bar of customers on his own.

Kyle raised an eyebrow, unable to let this opportunity slide. "Here I thought you knew everything there was to know about running this place."

Ryan's jaw set but he said nothing as he pushed past Kyle into the pub, where already the Friday afternoon crowd had gathered, and Kyle wasted no time in slipping out the front door and onto Main Street, brightly lit by the warm sun, a stark contrast to the darkness of the bar. It took a moment for his eyes to adjust, to take in the flowerpots flanking doors and the couples walking hand in hand on the sidewalks or sitting on the wrought-iron benches.

He didn't recognize half the faces, which meant tourism season had started, even if it didn't officially kick off until Memorial Day weekend, which was still weeks away. Either way, change was in the air.

And maybe, for once, he was ready for it.

He half expected Brooke not to show up tonight, and when he reached the ice cream shop and pulled open the door, he was surprised to see her sitting at a corner table, a little smile on her pretty mouth as she met his eye. She fluttered her fingers in a wave, and he pulled in a breath, realizing that he'd forgotten that simple gesture, or maybe, blocked it out. But now, seeing her so casually waving to him as she had all those other times, he was right back there. To this same town. Same storefront.

For a moment, he almost forgot they weren't married anymore.

He resisted the urge to reach down and greet her with a hug or a kiss or some sort of affection. Instead, he approached the table and grinned, while she blinked up at him pleasantly, if, he realized with a heaviness in his chest, maybe with a bit of impatience.

She didn't want to be here.

And that was all the more reason to see this through. It was his only chance to nail her down, talk things out in a way they never had before.

It was his last chance.

"It's filling up quickly," Brooke said, motioning to the room. "I thought I'd get us a table."

"You picked a good one," he said, omitting the fact that it was their usual table, back when they used to come here together. Had she chosen it on purpose?

From the controlled flatness of her expression, he doubted it.

"I'll get our orders," he said.

"Raspberry—"

He smiled broader. "I remember."

He remembered everything: the brand of shampoo she used and the way it smelled, leaving a scent on her pillow that he never wanted to wash away; the sound of her laugh when she talked with her sisters, the way her arms felt when she slid them around his waist and pulled him close. And that was just the problem. Early on, in the months after she'd first left, he still stiffened every time the door to the pub opened, expecting to see her walking through, her blue eyes gleaming, her smile radiant, waiting for her to plant a kiss on his mouth before excitedly telling him about an apartment she found in her internet search or a spot in New York they'd have to try once they got there. They'd talk about it every evening, too, sitting side by side on the chairs he'd carved, looking out over the lake, dreaming of the life they'd have together.

But there was no New York, not for him. And she never did walk through the door again. Or plant a kiss on his mouth. So why was it that he could still feel it like it was yesterday?

He placed the order, hoping that Brooke was in a better mood when he returned to the table. He didn't like the strain, not then, not now. It wasn't how it was ever supposed to turn out for them.

Five minutes later, he returned to the table, just in time to catch a woman's eye as she grabbed some extra napkins from the service station near the back wall. He realized with an internal groan that it was Jackie Walker, easily the chattiest classmate from first through twelfth grade.

"Brooke!" Her eyes popped in surprise. "Brooke Conway? I thought that was you!"

Brooke stood up and greeted Jackie with equal warmness, leaning in for a hug before resuming her seat. It didn't go unnoticed by Kyle that Brooke hadn't given him the same warm greeting. Not even given a handshake, even though that would have been...weird. But then, everything about this was weird. He was sitting across the table from his wife. His wife! And he didn't know anything about the last six years of her life at all.

"I'm only in town for the weekend," Jackie went on. "Thought I'd finally show my kids where I grew up. My goodness, since my parents moved away, I haven't been back!"

Evidently, Jackie was out of the loop since moving away. She had no idea that Brooke herself had just returned.

"Oh! It's so good to see the two of you. When was that wedding again?"

"Six years ago this June," Kyle stated.

"Six years! Of course, right before my parents moved. Most couples don't make it that far nowadays." Jackie clucked. "But then, you two were a perfect match. Cute as buttons. Pretty as a picture. And Brooke was the most beautiful bride."

"She certainly was," Kyle agreed.

He saw Brooke firm her mouth. Clearly, she wasn't finding any of this half as amusing as he was.

"Any kids?" Jackie asked. She blinked at them, expecting an answer.

Kyle coughed, only entertaining a moment of panic that while he didn't have children, it was possible that...but no. No, surely he would have heard word about Steve and Miriam Conway having a grandchild.

He needed to get a grip. He may not have been face to face with Brooke for almost six years, but that didn't mean he didn't know her. He did know her. He knew every inch of her. He knew her dreams, her goals, and her biggest secret.

And he knew her heart. After all, he'd had it once.

"No kids!" Kyle grinned broadly, playing along. "Yet."

He felt Brooke's kick under the table. Her eyes glimmered against her frozen smile.

"Just...focused on our careers," she said tightly.

Careers. The word felt sour to his ears, and he licked his cone, hoping that Jackie would get the hint. Fortunately, a tow-headed boy with an ice cream stain down the front of his striped shirt called out impatiently from the doorway before closing it again.

Jackie gave an apologetic shrug and said, "Duty calls. Better run before they get into trouble! It was so good seeing the two of you again!"

"Why did you entertain her?" Brooke accused the moment Jackie was out of earshot.

Kyle shrugged. He was still staving off a grin as he bit into his cone. "What would you rather me have said? That my blushing bride bolted the moment things got rough? Or that this is our first night out as a married couple since a couple of months after our wedding day?"

"You're making it out to sound like it's all my fault," Brooke said.

"Isn't it?" He pulled in a breath, told himself to get a hold of his emotions. This wasn't what tonight was supposed to be about. It was supposed to be a chance for the two of them to catch up, even reconnect a little. It wasn't supposed to end in an argument.

"Well, it seems like we've had no problem sliding right back into the place where we last left off," Brooke said wryly, but there was hurt in her eyes that matched the heaviness in his chest. She poked at her ice cream with her spoon, and Kyle watched as the color rose in her cheeks. He'd upset her. And that wasn't his intention.

Truth be told, he didn't know what his intention was. Or why he'd thought this was a good idea. He only knew that signing some papers, now, when she'd only just returned, was a worse one.

"Let's go for a walk," he suggested, nudging his chin toward the door.

Brooke shook her head. "Uh-uh. You asked me to meet you for ice cream, and here I am." She took a huge bite, causing her cheeks to bulge.

He narrowed his eyes. "Is this one of those ice-cream eating contests that they sometimes have at the local festivals?" he asked with a little laugh, but then it hit him. She was trying to speed things up. To get away. Again.

And that hurt. More than it probably should.

*

Eventually, Kyle managed to convince her to take a walk. Or rather, circumstances convinced her, when Chrissy Roberts walked into the parlor, and Brooke very much doubted that in the time she'd been away Chrissy had changed her ways. She'd always been a gossip, ever since she was editor of the school newspaper and added a "happenings" column to the front page. There was no telling what she'd have to say if she spotted Brooke and Kyle sitting at the corner table, enjoying an ice cream on a warm Friday evening. Probably more than Jackie had said, that was a given.

Really, what had she expected? She was back in Blue Harbor, and even though she and Kyle were long over, here at least, they would always be connected.

They managed to slip away unnoticed, or so Brooke hoped. Still, it took some dodging and hiding behind some of the taller members of the community who were waiting in line, studying the menu on the board, unaware that they were being used as human shields.

Both Brooke and Kyle were laughing by the time they hit the sidewalk. The release of nervous energy felt good.

"The last thing I needed was another round of interrogation," Brooke said, shaking her head.

"You mean you don't like everyone knowing if you have kids and why you don't, and if you're going to get married again, or if you're still married?" Kyle's grin was wry and against her better judgment, she felt a kinship with him.

"Some things never change," Brooke said.

"No, some things don't." Kyle was giving her a funny look, and she wished she could polish off the ice cream, but Kyle had bought the largest size and she was already getting full, and besides, she still hadn't gotten to the point of the night. At least, not her point of it.

"Some things do, though," she said airily, trying to look the other way. They were heading down Main Street now, toward the town square, and she wasn't sure whether she hoped to see one of her friends or family members or be spared. What was worse? Explaining what was going on when she didn't even know herself and couldn't exactly admit the truth, or being alone with Kyle again?

She didn't like being alone with him. Didn't like the way her stomach pulled when she met his eye. The way her heart tugged when she caught his grin.

That it felt good to share a laugh. That maybe that wasn't all that felt good.

"I mean, I'm not the same person I was six years ago," she said firmly. Time had passed. They'd moved on. At least she had.

Whereas Kyle…He was exactly where he'd always been.

"In what ways?" he asked as they neared a bench and sat down. It was the same bench they'd always sat on when they came to this park, and she told herself that it was because it was the only one currently unoccupied. Strange coincidence, nothing more. Just life reminding her of a different time. A different path, perhaps.

"Well, I've learned that I can do things on my own." When she caught the injury in his eyes, she added, "Without my family helping me. I mean, I appreciate their help, and I'm happy to be back here with them, but it was important for me to learn to stand on my own."

He nodded thoughtfully. "Enough to open your own successful business."

"We'll see about that." She stirred her melting ice cream, hating the doubt that had crept into her voice. She was excited about her shop, about the prospect of full creative control, but she still couldn't shake her final experience in New York.

She forced a smile as she scooped more ice cream into her mouth. As expected, Kyle was frowning a little. She didn't need him of all people to see her waver.

"Once the loan comes through I'll really be able to do what I want with the business," she said firmly, getting back on track. She thought of her business plan, her checklist. If she could stick to it, she'd be okay. She'd be safe.

"And what is that exactly?"

She supposed there was no secret to hold onto, and she was happy to keep the topic neutral. "Fabric is expensive, especially for wedding gowns, and a lot of material is usually used. Then there are the bridal shows I'd like to be a part of, and advertising isn't free either. I'll need to hire an assistant if I ever want to take a day off without closing the store."

He gave a little smile. "You always dreamed big."

"Is there any other way?" She held his gaze for a moment, feeling her stomach flutter, and then looked away. She realized that her hands were shaking.

"Those are big plans, but it sounds like you know what you want." He nodded slowly. "It would be a large loan, I assume."

"One that would be difficult to qualify for given your position," she said delicately. She hated talking about that pub. She knew why he'd felt the need to hold onto it, but she didn't understand why he didn't feel the same need to hold onto her, too. "Restaurants are risky," she added quickly. Surely he knew that.

He raised his eyebrows, saying nothing.

She looked back at her ice cream, sadness pulling at her chest for the situations that had brought them to this point. Two strangers with a shared past, sitting on a bench, eating ice cream, thinking about all that might have been.

Jackie's comments had stung, of course. Kids. Would they have had kids if she'd stayed behind? When they'd talked about starting a family, it felt far off and distant. Something they would have done once they were more settled in their careers. After they'd done what they'd set out to do in the big city.

A time like now, she realized.

Brooke felt her stomach knot and she force-fed herself more ice cream, trying to push away the thought. There was no use in playing out different scenarios. Their decisions had been made.

There was no use in being here at all.

She polished off her last scoop, even though she felt almost sick from the sugar. "Well, this was…" She couldn't say it was nice. She really couldn't say what it was. She just knew that it was confusing and that she wanted to leave, to go home, and not think about Kyle for a while. It had been so much easier in New York.

"Next time I'll have to choose something a little farther out of the center of town and away from prying eyes," Kyle said, and she felt her stomach drop.

"Next time?" She squared him with a look. A hard one.

He rose slowly. "You promised me six. That was the deal."

"Kyle." She was pleading. She couldn't even believe that he'd want to get together again when this was so awkward, so...difficult.

"Six. This was one." There was enough authority in his tone to remind her who had the upper hand.

Her heart was torn between confusion, anger, and compassion. "Why are you doing this, Kyle?" she asked softly. "We both know that we're not right for each other. Would you really refuse to sign the papers if I had them drawn up?"

His expression was unreadable. Finally, he said, "Maybe."

She stared at him. Would he contest the divorce? And for what reason?

Punishment, she realized. For going to New York without him.

"So this is payback. I knew it. For me leaving you." She shook her head, feeling all those old frustrations come running back at full speed.

"So you admit that you left me," he said, rolling back on his heels, his look appraising. "I've been wondering why you seem so mad at me when I'm not the one who ended things."

"You ended everything, Kyle!"

He lifted an eyebrow as if he was curious by her rendition of the story.

She sputtered on her words, blinking quickly, trying to form a coherent defense. Did he not see his part in any of this?

"We had plans," she finally said.

"We had *vows*," he countered, silencing her. Finally, he dropped his shoulders and said, "Looks like we'll have plenty to discuss at our next date."

"Meet-up," she corrected.

"Whatever you want to call it," he said with a friendly shrug that was downright infuriating. "But you agree? You'll come?"

"Fine," she huffed. Because just like last time, he hadn't left her any other choice.

7

Bella's Books was tucked on Main Street behind a blossoming tree whose petals were covering the wrought-iron bench below. Just the sight of it made Brooke smile, and she made a mental note to think about ways to incorporate those delicate flowers into a gown for next spring—something cascading and youthful, perfect for a younger client.

Something her old boss would have had another word for: trite. Overdone. Or already done. Or too ambitious. That was the one that always stung the most. Too ambitious. Perhaps because it hit the deepest wound, that she cared too much. Enough to leave her town. Her husband. That she didn't have what it took. That she was trying too hard and didn't belong.

Well, now she was right where she belonged, wasn't she? She was a small-town girl at heart and this was still her home. And the new client from Pine Falls wouldn't be asking about doing her bridesmaid gowns if she didn't think Brooke had what it took.

For a moment, Brooke felt better. And with that thought tucked away, she vowed not to think about work anymore tonight—or Kyle, who was forever creeping up into the forefront of her mind, especially since last night.

It was book club, and she had promised to attend, even if she hadn't read the novel. She knew these clubs were often an excuse for the women in town to gather, though some would take it more seriously, like her sister Gabby. It was exactly what she needed—a night with her sisters and cousins and old friends and neighbors that she hadn't yet bumped into on her quick errands around town.

Brooke transferred the wine bottle she'd purchased on the way over into her tote and opened the door, immediately greeted by the buzz of laughter and conversation, and the smells of fresh baked goods.

She breathed a sigh of relief. This was one thing she'd never found in New York and never could. Family, friends, a community.

And... "Candy!" The door had barely closed behind her and already she was being pulled in for a long hug.

"Oh, I heard you were coming tonight! I swear, that sister of yours has been eyeing the door for the last ten minutes waiting for you."

Brooke glanced at Gabby over Candy's shoulder and gave her a conspiratorial wink. Gabby took a long slug of wine and refilled her glass.

"I was just telling Gabby that I have a new idea for my flowers," Candy exclaimed, releasing her.

Brooke raised an eyebrow, but her sister didn't catch her eye. She wasn't surprised. A woman with as many ideas as Candy was bound to change her mind many times before her big day, and it was one reason why she hadn't committed too much time to her sketches just yet.

"And I was wondering," Candy said, looking suddenly very serious. "What do you think of a mermaid-style dress?"

Brooke blinked several times. Beside her, she heard Gabby's wine bubble. No doubt her sister was trying to smother a laugh in her glass.

Brooke managed not to sigh and tilted her head politely. "I thought we left off at a full ballgown." There were many, many other ideas when it came to fabric and the bodice and the sleeve-length, but the actual cut of the dress was something that Brooke had nailed down on Wednesday. Or so she'd thought.

Candy pressed a finger to her mouth. "Mmm. Yes. But then I thought...these curves." She ran her hands over her hips and gave a little eyebrow wiggle. "Why not *accentuate* them?"

Now Gabby had to walk away, all pink in the cheeks and shoulders shaking, while Brooke was left to deal with Candy on her own.

She paused, trying to be tactful. "Let's think about it, Candy. We have time."

Not much if she was left with a redesign at the final hour, but Brooke was confident that once she designed something that Candy loved, there would be no second-guessing. "I always think that you shouldn't compete with the gown. That the bride should still be the focal point."

Candy stared at her in wonder. "I knew that you would be the best designer for my dress. Oh, I can't wait to see what you come up with!" She squealed, before noticing someone over Brooke's shoulder and wiggling her fingers. "Oh, it's Helena! I need to talk to her about my late charge at the library again."

Brooke looked over her shoulder at her former classmate, who was now the strictest librarian the town had known in three generations, or so her sisters told her. Brooke wondered if she had loosened up over the years, but judging from her stern expression as Candy seemed to plead with words like "enraptured" and "couldn't part with it when it was due back," Helena hadn't changed one bit.

But then, what did she expect? This was Blue Harbor, and much of the town, and its residents, were exactly as she'd left them.

Including Kyle.

"I have a confession," she said to Gabby when she joined her at the back of the room.

"Let me guess? You're regretting having a part in Candy's wedding day? Join the club."

Brooke laughed. Candy was probably a good test. There would be many other indecisive or picky brides to contend with down the road.

"No," she said, helping herself to a glass of wine from the tray that was set up on the table. "Something else."

"Oh?" The excitement that flashed in Gabby's eyes was a foreshadowing of how her sister would react if she were to ever find out Brooke's real secret, and it was confirmation that it was best never to reveal it. Besides, in a matter of weeks, there would be nothing to tell. Papers would be signed. The marriage would officially be over.

Brooke didn't know why that filled her with a sense of sadness. The relationship had been over for years.

"Something juicy?" Gabby's eyes downright twinkled. She loved drama too much for her own good, and the fiction she devoured was no doubt partly to blame.

"Sorry to disappoint you," Brooke said wryly. She dropped her voice to a whisper. "I didn't have time to read the book. I just...skimmed the first chapter."

Gabby looked slightly disappointed but waved her hand through the air. "I'm probably the only person who read the book, other than Bella, of course. We might discuss it for a few minutes, and seeing as it's your first meeting and you did just open a business, you have a free pass to be a wallflower. But...I have a feeling the real topic of conversation tonight will be your return!"

Gabby was right about that, as several former classmates turned to spot her and immediately cross the room. Brooke greeted them all warmly—it was nice to be back with people who knew her—except for the part of her life that she'd rather not remember.

Turning the conversation off herself, she motioned to Sadie Henderick's baby bump, and said, "I can't even believe you're going to be a mother!"

"Number two," Sadie said with a casual smile.

Two? Brooke realized that this could have been her life, if she'd stayed behind, living with Kyle, going about the routine of married life. And what would that have been like? Would she have worked for Patsy, selling other people's clothes, maybe dabbling in a few designs of her own, while Kyle tended bar at Harrison's and eventually gave up on the custom furniture that he had once put such pride and effort into creating?

"And what about you, Brooke?" another classmate from school asked. Brooke couldn't help but notice the rings on her left hand as she sipped her white wine. "Did you find love in the big city?"

Brooke gave a wan smile. "I dated here and there, but..." *But I'm still legally married.* She bit her lip to hide her smile. Wouldn't that put an end to this conversation, and fast?

She composed herself and said, "But work kept me busy."

"And why give it all up?" Sadie wanted to know.

Brooke could see there was no malice in the question, only idle curiosity. She'd prepared herself for this, knowing how Blue Harbor could be, small enough to be overly familiar, especially when you wanted to guard some information.

She gave a bigger smile and rehearsed her excuse: "I missed my family, and when the opportunity came about to open my own boutique, it was too good to pass up."

It was true in many ways, she thought, her shoulders sagging in relief as Gabby refilled her wine glass without having to be asked. She didn't have to ask her sister the blend—they only bought and drank the Conway brand out of loyalty.

And it was that exact loyalty that prompted Gabby to give her a subtle wink and then say, "You won't mind if I whisk my sister away, ladies. Bella's friend had some questions about wedding gowns. And have you seen Brooke's designs? Stunning! I'm recommending her to anyone who comes into my shop asking about flowers."

"It's almost a shame we're already married!" The women laughed.

Gabby's lids hooded as she led Brooke across the small room to a circle of chairs that Bella had set up in the children's area.

"Thank you," Brooke whispered gratefully.

"If you thought that was rough, I have to write out the cards their husbands send them every Valentine's Day." Gabby sighed. "Honestly, why haven't I found true love yet?"

Brooke looked at her sister squarely. "You want the real answer or the one that you tell yourself?"

Gabby pinched her lips. She knew that Brooke had a point.

"You're too picky," Brooke summarized, and it was true. Gabby was a beauty, but she was also funny, quick, and passionate about her opinions and her career. And she was entirely too discriminating when it came to men, especially in a town without much selection.

Not that this excuse could hold for much longer. As Gabby had pointed out, all these other women were finding love. And there were plenty of handsome men in town, too.

Her mind drifted to Kyle and she quickly pulled it back again.

Gabby sighed. "Can I help it if I'm selective? Besides, name someone. Name a single guy other than Jackson that might be a good match for me."

"I haven't been back in a while. What about…Richard—"

Before she could even finish, Gabby cut her off. "Moved away about three years ago. Name another."

Brooke sipped her wine and tried to think. "What about Chri—"

Again, Gabby shook her head. "Engaged to someone from Chicago."

Brooke was getting exasperated. Gabby was trying to prove a point. "Well, there's Ryan—"

Gabby stared at her in shock. "Ryan *Harrison*? But he's Kyle's brother!"

Of course. Loyalty and all that. Brooke gave her sister a smile of encouragement. "Not every guy is like the hero in those books you read. They're human, with flaws, just like you and me. Nothing will ever be perfect and you'll be alone a long time if you're waiting for it to be. Relationships take hard work and compromise."

Gabby arched a brow and gave her a knowing look. "No offense, Brooke, but isn't that the same advice that Mom gave you right before you moved to New York?"

Shoot. It was. And Brooke hadn't heeded it, had she?

She frowned. "That was different. Kyle and I had a plan and he changed course at the last minute."

Gabby nodded. She knew the story, of course. Knew it well. It was comforting that Brooke didn't need to explain anything to her. Still, she could tell by the way Gabby was squinting her eyes as she sipped her wine that this subject wasn't dropped just yet.

"Do you ever wonder if you'd have been happy if you hadn't moved, though?" When Brooke started to object, Gabby held up a hand. "Hear me out. You're back now. You have that lovely boutique, sure. But maybe you still could have ended up right there, in that storefront, with your beautiful creations, without..."

"Without ruining my marriage?" Brooke felt her defenses flare up along with the heat in her cheeks.

Gabby winced. "I wouldn't have worded it that way, but...you were so in love."

"We were," Brooke said crisply. She drank back a long sip of her wine, followed by another. "But Kyle made a choice, Gabby. He could have come with me, and instead, he let me go."

"I guess you're right," Gabby sighed as she sauntered away to raid the buffet of snacks, but the look in her eyes when she turned back told Brooke that she didn't mean a word of that, and Brooke wasn't in the mood to argue.

Or think about Kyle. Instead, she forced herself to look around the room, at the display tables of new releases, to the stacked shelves organized by category, to the cozy armchairs and brass reading lamps and sconces that made the room feel well lit but not overly bright, like the kind of place you might want to stay for a while.

It was quintessential Blue Harbor—inviting and warm, and quaint. It was everything the city hadn't been and never would be.

And it was filled with people who knew her.

A little too well in some cases, she thought, eyeing her sister across the room.

"Penny for your thoughts." Bella sidled up to her. "And you cannot get away with standing here all by yourself when so many people here want to see you."

Brooke suddenly felt very tired. "Long week," she said with a weak smile. And a more emotionally draining one than she'd even feared.

She glanced around the room at the familiar faces. She didn't want to talk about New York anymore, or why she'd moved back, because no matter how much she spun the story that she wanted to open her own boutique, and despite the pride she did feel, another part of her was overwhelmed with doubt.

"Well, don't worry. I'm about to gather everyone into the circle anyway. I have a feeling if I don't, Candy will make the rounds and I might lose a few guests before the discussion starts." She laughed in a non-menacing way. It seemed that everyone understood that Candy had a strong personality.

"She's only here because tonight's pick was a romance," Gabby said, joining them.

"Then you have nothing to complain about!" Brooke knew that romance was Gabby's favorite genre.

Gabby gave a little shrug. "Other than the fact that the only romance I seem to find is in the pages of my books, or on the cards I write for my flower deliveries...to other people."

Brooke sympathized, even if she wasn't looking for love herself. It wasn't always easy to see other people find it. And keep it.

Gabby jutted her chin. "Uh-oh. Looks like Helena is getting worked up. You know she's this close to banning Candy from checking out any more books."

Bella grinned. "Good. More business for me." She looked over her shoulder and blew out a breath. "Yikes. I see what you mean. Okay, we'll start early tonight."

Brooke was happy when Bella asked everyone to take their seats. She took a chair near the back, hoping to slip out as soon as the discussion ended. She needed a good night's sleep because she had a feeling that until her next five meet-ups with Kyle were over and done with, she wouldn't be finding much rest at all.

*

Brooke stepped out onto the sidewalk, feeling the first few drops of rain land on her head. She looked up at the sky; it was overcast, the sidewalks empty, the only light coming from the warmly lit windows of the small inns that lined Main Street and the lampposts that glowed high above.

She knew enough about the weather patterns to quicken her step as the rain began to fall stronger. Her apartment wasn't far, and she shivered in her sweater as the rain soaked her skin. A hot cup of tea and some warm pajamas were moments away. She just had to hop over that puddle, and—

"Those aren't the most weather appropriate shoes, are they?" A deep voice cut through her thoughts.

Brooke turned to see Kyle grinning back at her, under the comfortable shield of a large umbrella.

Brooke didn't need to look at her feet to know what he was referring to, but she did it anyway, as an excuse to break his stare. The butterflies remained in her stomach even still, fluttering away as she considered her next words.

Was this so easy for him, or was he…

No. She shook that thought away immediately. There was no way that Kyle Harrison was flirting with her. If he still had feelings for her, he'd had a long time to make them known.

To her dismay, her cognac leather wedges were getting soaked, and she cursed herself for not checking the weather forecast earlier.

"I should hurry," she said, seizing the opportunity.

But she was too late. Kyle had closed the distance between them, and now his umbrella was over her head, his arm pressing against her back in an overly familiar way. Under the shield of the fabric, she could feel the heat of his body, smell the musk of his skin and the faint scent of spice from his cologne. The same one he always wore. How many nights had she curled next to him in bed, her head on his chest, breathing in this smell, lulled by the beating of his heart?

The rain was falling harder now, making it impossible to break away. Damn it.

"I'm happy I ran into you," he said, and she could hear the grin in his voice, even though she refused to look up at him. It was bad enough that he practically had his arm around her as they walked toward her shop. "I didn't like the way we left things."

"Me either," she admitted after a pause. Feeling the need to explain, she pressed, "I don't want us to hurt anymore. I don't want to be upset by the past. I...just want to move on."

He nodded, kept walking, slowly. Too slowly. He was setting the pace.

"I'm surprised you aren't at the pub," she said, trying to steer the conversation away from their relationship.

He didn't say anything for a beat, and they approached the corner, checked for cars. As luck would have it, a few were approaching, their headlights strong, making it impossible to gauge their distance or speed, because if she had it her way, she'd make a run for it. Anything to get away from Kyle, his arm, his body...

"Is Ryan planning to stay on?" She hadn't considered such a thing before, but who was she to assume otherwise? People changed. Relationships did too. She should know.

"Ryan moved back because he had a break-up, and I think he needs to sort some stuff out, personally. Unfortunately, that means he has time on his hands and he's decided to stick his nose into my business. Well, the family business. Ryan and I...Well, you know."

Yes. She did. They'd always been opposites. One creative, one analytical. Both stubborn to a fault, not that she'd be saying that. She wasn't in the mood to argue tonight and talking about the past stirred up feelings she'd rather forget.

Still, a part of her softened as they finally made their way across the intersection. "I'm sure your father would be pleased to see both his sons working together at the family business."

This time, she felt his body stiffen behind her, and she wondered if she'd hit a nerve. She looked up to see his jaw locked, his eyes focused straight ahead, and she realized that she had.

"I know your feelings about the pub if that's what you're getting at," he said.

"I didn't mean it that way," she said honestly. "I meant...I know how much that pub meant to your father. And I know how much you did, too."

She held her breath, waiting for a defensive retort, wondering why she was even bothering to bring up these old conversations. Because they weren't finished, she concluded, as they neared her front door. Because everything that had been said all those years ago had been said in hurt and anger and now, after all this time, some of it was still there.

Kyle's father did love that pub. But he loved Kyle more. And she knew that this wasn't what he would have wanted, even if that was what Kyle had always thought.

Maybe for the best, Kyle didn't let the topic go any further. "He was a good man," was all he said.

Brooke nodded. "How's your mother?"

"Good," he replied, his voice more relaxed. "She stays busy with her charity groups and volunteer activity."

Mrs. Harrison had always been welcoming to Brooke, saying she was the first daughter she'd ever had. How was that for guilt? But she had also encouraged Kyle to pursue his dreams, to live his life, as planned.

Even now, Brooke could still remember Kyle's response to that: "Plans changed."

Yes, Brooke thought sadly. They had. Then, and now.

She was relieved to see that her shop window was nearly within reach now, the dress in the window lit up by a string of fairy lights she'd draped over the base of the bay window.

"Well, I should get out of these wet clothes."

She caught the quirk of his mouth and immediately regretted her choice of words.

She pinched her mouth as she fished for her key, which seemed to have sunk to the bottom of her oversized tote.

"Need any help?" he asked.

"You've helped enough for one night," she replied, gripping the metal object at the bottom of the bag. Her hands fumbled as she jammed it through the old-fashioned keyhole. Darn thing stuck every time.

She turned, giving him one last, tight smile, hating the way her heart sped up at the sight of his face, so close to hers, so patient. So handsome. No other man had ever made her stomach flip over the way he did.

Puppy love, she told herself. First love. They have a lasting impression, however impractical.

"Thank you for the umbrella," she said as she heard the lock click. The door pushed open. Freedom was only a staircase away.

But from the look in his eyes, Kyle wasn't quite finished with the night.

Perhaps, she realized, by the way her chest was rising and falling with each breath, she wasn't either.

It had never been easy to walk away from Kyle. And never without looking back.

"We have to schedule our next *meet-up*," he said, emphasizing his word choice from yesterday.

"I would think tonight counts as something," she said.

With raised eyebrows, he motioned down the street to the bookshop. "A walk from here to there? Sorry, hon, that's par for the course living in such a small town. Bound to happen…countless times."

Countless times? She realized this was probably true. That even after their meet-ups were over and done with, she wouldn't be free of him. She'd just be….free. Free to move on. Marry again.

She swallowed hard, not liking that thought. It was one thing to know they had each moved on. It was another to witness it.

Feeling the need to protect herself, she folded her arms across her chest.

"What did you have in mind?"

"I was thinking we'd go to Firefly Café."

"The café?" She didn't know if she should be relieved or horrified that it was now owned by her cousin Amelia. Amelia was a trusting type, not prone to gossip or speculation, but she would be undoubtedly curious—who wouldn't be? And much like the pub at the Carriage House Inn, the café was very popular. "I thought you said we'd go somewhere less…crowded." Instantly, she regretted saying anything.

He raised an eyebrow. "Something just the two of us? And here I thought you were still so eager to get away from me."

She sighed. "Fine. The café."

"The café," he said with a nod. "Tuesday night special is shrimp and grits. Amelia kept the tradition going when she took over."

If he was trying to bribe her, it wouldn't work, even if her mouth did water at the prospect of one of her favorite dishes that used to be made by the former owner of the restaurant. She could enjoy it on her own, without his company.

Only right now, that didn't seem like much of an option.

"I don't see much point in arguing." If they walked in together, then it would most certainly raise eyebrows. "What are we supposed to tell people who are surprised to see us together?"

"You mean they don't all know we're still married?"

Seeing the look of shock on her face, he burst out laughing. It was a loud, rumbling sound, and one that she'd missed, oh so much.

She couldn't help but smile, knowing now that he had been teasing her.

"So Ryan doesn't know?" She assumed that if Kyle's mother knew the truth, it would have gotten back to her own family by now. Their mothers were friendly.

Kyle gave a look that showed he didn't care. "They all assumed the obvious. I never bothered to set the record straight. The way I see it, what happened between you and me is between us. And I'd like it to stay that way. So if we want to go to dinner, then we'll go to dinner."

And he wanted to go to dinner. She pulled in a breath, anxiety kicking in when she realized she was mildly flattered by this, that a part of him still cared. That maybe, he always had, even when she'd assumed he didn't.

"Seven o'clock?" His grin was cocky, not much different than it had been back in high school when she'd first started to notice him in a new, exciting way.

"As good a time as any, I suppose," she said, tossing up her hands.

He shoved his free hand in his pocket, seeming amused by her lack of enthusiasm, as he backed away, into the rain. "Don't worry, I promise to make it worth your while, and at least you know you'll be getting a good meal out of it."

There was only one thing she wanted out of another tense evening with Kyle, but she kept her mouth shut and nodded in agreement. "Tuesday it is then."

By then she'd be a third of the way through the terms of their agreement. And one step closer to her goal.

Eye on the prize, she reminded herself as she trudged up the dark stairs to her empty apartment.

8

On Tuesday night, Brooke checked the clock for the tenth time in as many minutes, reluctantly set her sketches for Candy's wedding gown to the side, smoothed her hair, and slipped into a pale pink blouse and jeans that were far more comfortable than the pencil skirt and heels she'd been wearing for the past eight hours.

Her apartment was coming together, now that her remaining belongings had all been delivered, but she was yet to make it feel like home. The tall windows would benefit from long drapes, and she saw little sense in buying some when she could make her own. A few throw pillows for the bed might help, and, considering that her space was nearly quadruple the size of her New York apartment, she might browse the shops in town for a coffee table and armchair.

Maybe her mother would even be willing to part with a few things from the attic—Brooke wasn't afraid to tackle a reupholstery project.

She nearly laughed at herself, and she could hear her mother doing the same. As if she didn't have enough on her plate with getting her business off the ground. She hadn't sat at her sewing machine since opening the doors, even though she'd hoped to continue to make sample gowns for clients who wanted to purchase something off the rack. But keeping busy kept her mind busy. And the sooner this apartment felt like home, the better.

Maybe it would make her stop thinking of the other place in town that had once been her home.

With a sigh, she grabbed her tote and walked to the café, which took all of five minutes, even if she did practically drag herself there, and stop to look in every single shop window until she met the path down to the lakefront.

She was early, but it beat sitting around the apartment, dreading the thought of an evening with Kyle almost as much as she felt anticipation toward it. Remembering that Maddie's new bakery was just next door to Firefly Café, she decided to pop in for a cup of coffee beforehand.

Buttercream Bakery was as beautiful as anything she had seen in all her years of living in New York, and she wasn't shy in telling her cousin so the moment she spotted her.

"You should come in one morning when we're fully stocked," Maddie said, pointing to the nearly empty bakery case. "We're pretty picked over by the dinner hour, but once I have more help, I think we'll stay open later a few nights a week."

"Growing as you go then?" It was the same strategy Brooke had for herself, but then, she and Maddie had both learned from the best, hadn't they? They'd watched their fathers work together to take over the orchard and grow it into what it was today. And Britt was taking it one step further now that she was running operations—a future generation of Conway women, taking the town by its reins.

She smiled at that. It felt good. Comfortable. And no matter what her peers back in Manhattan might say, it felt like an accomplishment.

"I'm trying," Maddie admitted. Her eyebrows shot up. "It was a little daunting at first. Big shoes to fill and all."

Brooke was relieved to hear that she wasn't alone with these feelings. She'd started to wonder if she'd ever find time to sew the dresses she'd been commissioned to make if she was busy tending to customers all day—not that she could complain about this. From the looks of the bakery, demand was not an issue for Maddie either.

"Nearly every table is filled," she commented. "You're doing something right."

She wanted to believe the same for herself, but it was hard to shake the words of her former boss. The belief that she had bigger aspirations than she was capable of fulfilling.

"So long as people keep coming back, I tell myself that," Maddie said with a shrug. "But that first week was certainly nerve-racking."

"Tell me about it," Brooke confessed. "I see how Gabby can run her business in her sleep and I don't know how she does it. I still jump every time the door to my shop opens!"

"So do I!" Maddie burst out laughing, and Brooke joined in. It was a good, hearty laugh, the kind that stayed with you, the good feelings lasting long after the moment had passed. It was the reason she had come back here. The reason she would stay.

The reason why it is was worth suffering through one more meeting with Kyle. She was a busy woman; surely he had to respect that. Just like he'd have to accept that there was no point to these little get-togethers. She'd see to that tonight.

"What can I get you?" Maddie scanned the half-empty plates of scones, brownies, and cookies. "I have one more double chocolate chip?"

It was tempting, but Brooke shook her head. "Another day. Tonight I'll just have coffee. I'm going over to the café for dinner." The thought of seeing Kyle again filled her with dread.

"With Gabby? I'm closing up soon and I didn't have time to stop for lunch. I could meet you guys in a bit? Shrimp and grits is the special on Tuesdays this month."

So she'd heard. Brooke would have loved nothing more than to have a lighthearted meal with her sister and cousin, so much so that she made a mental note to do that soon. "I'm not meeting Gabby."

She paused, wondering how she could even explain her reason for meeting Kyle. As far as everyone in town knew, their marriage had ended—in every possible way—years ago. That there was nothing left between them to even discuss.

"Oh? One of your friends from school then?" Maddie asked conversationally as she filled a mug with coffee.

Again, a nice idea, and much more appealing than the thought of sitting across from her ex—or not so ex—husband for an hour.

And it had better not be more than an hour.

She pulled in a breath. "Kyle asked to meet me."

Maddie's eyes went round. She didn't blink for several seconds. "Kyle? Why?"

Good question, Brooke thought ruefully. She felt her eyes hood. "I think he just wants to make sure things are civil between us, with me being back in town and everything."

It was partially true, she figured, and maybe that would be one good outcome from all of this. In a town this small, it would be much easier if everyone could get along.

Maddie seemed to relax and nodded her head. "That makes sense. But...it won't be awkward?"

Brooke raised an eyebrow. "Oh, it will be awkward all right."

She laughed, and Maddie laughed too, and for a brief, fuzzy moment, she didn't feel so alone in the world. She had someone on her side. A lot of them, actually.

But not Kyle, she thought. He was the one person who was supposed to be on her side, and who had let her down instead.

*

Kyle was already seated at a table near the window when Brooke walked into the café a few moments later through the arched doorway that connected Maddie's bakery to Amelia's establishment. Long ago, the café had been owned by another woman, and Brooke was happy that her cousin had decided to keep the restaurant going under a new name. These were the types of places that made coming back to Blue Harbor easier. It helped to know that some things hadn't changed in her absence.

But Kyle…well, he hadn't changed either, and Brooke didn't know what to make of that. Would she have been happier to hear that he'd met someone, was planning to marry again, maybe start a family?

She'd managed not to think about that scenario any more than she stopped herself from picturing what he'd looked like on their wedding day, or the night he'd proposed, or countless other times that had become so routine they all blended together until the memories were no longer clear.

But now everything was very clear. Too clear. The sight of him made her pull a sharp intake of breath. She'd half expected jeans and a tee—something he wore to the pub, or at least had when she knew him. But tonight he was wearing a dress shirt, and his hair looked freshly combed, and she had to steady herself for a moment, thinking that he'd possibly dressed up for her. That she still mattered to him.

Because if she did…Well, she didn't quite know how to feel about that.

She glanced at the counter as she approached the table, seeing only an unfamiliar face that must be one of Amelia's part-time staff. Good. Another sweep of the room didn't reveal anyone she knew. It was a Tuesday night, so the café was quiet.

Maybe, it was too quiet.

Kyle's expression lifted and he stood as she approached. "I'd hoped to sit out on the deck, but the breeze is strong this evening and I know how you get cold."

She told herself not to read too far into that. It was true, she liked to have a sweater or scarf on her at all times because the lake effect here in Blue Harbor could be as tricky as air-conditioning when it came to staying comfortable. It was just one simple small detail about her, as common as, say, the color of her eyes.

She laughed away her nervous energy by motioning to her cardigan tucked into her bag. "You know me," she said in a joking voice before he caught her eye sharply.

"Every inch of you."

She pinched her mouth and took her seat, shifting uncomfortably as Kyle did the same. Face to face across the table from him for an entire meal. Her stomach dropped as she hooked her bag over the back of her chair.

"Amelia working tonight?" she asked, hoping to keep the conversation light, the topics far from personal.

"If she is, I didn't see her," Kyle said. After a beat, he added, "But I did see Candy."

She resisted a smile as their eyes locked, and his gleamed with familiar amusement.

"So you know Candy then?" Not that she should be surprised. This was a small town.

"She's made her presence around town known," he said mildly. "And I see her at the Sunday market sometimes."

The Sunday market was a tradition at Conway Orchard, a defining part of her week growing up when the entire family would gather to sell local produce and baked goods. She shouldn't be surprised that he still went, considering most of the town turned out at least once a month, though some came weekly. He had been close to her family, in the same grade as Amelia, and no one had any bad feelings toward him.

"I didn't realize you still went there," she commented.

"I still live in this town." He shrugged, his gaze locking hers. "Had to hold onto some things."

She felt her heart pick up speed until she looked away. "It seems my cousins have come to embrace the woman their father is marrying." Brooke looked at the menu, but she couldn't properly concentrate, even though she was eager to see what Amelia had done with the place. She set it back down, glancing at him. "People move on, I suppose."

"Have you?"

The question was so frank, and she was unprepared for it, that she sputtered on the water she'd just reached for.

"Are you asking if I'm in a relationship?" She felt hot in the cheeks now. He raised a single eyebrow. "Not...at the moment."

She stared at her menu, saying nothing more, and eventually, she heard Kyle say, "Me either, in case you were wondering."

She looked up, giving a tight smile. "I wasn't."

"Or in case you already knew." His mouth twitched.

She pulled in a breath and sat back against her chair. "It's a small town and all of my family lives here. I hear things, obviously. And last I knew our moms were still friends."

He nodded. "Good friends."

She gave him a wary look, not even sure why she was still curious about his recent life. "You mean to tell me that you never dated anyone seriously in all this time?"

"I guess I don't let go of things easily."

"You established that when you weren't willing to sell the pub," she replied before she could stop herself.

The silence was heavy, and Brooke looked at the counter, now desperate to see Candy or Amelia. Let them wonder what they would, so long as they saved her.

Alas, nothing. They must be in the kitchen.

"Candy is a client, actually," she said lightly, again hoping to steer the conversation back to common ground. "They're getting married in July."

"You'll be going to the wedding then?"

She stared at him as if she'd misheard him. "Of course. I'm family."

"Just wasn't sure you'd still be here."

"Of course I'll still be here. I'm—"

He held up a hand. "Here to stay."

"Is there going to be a problem with that?" She set the menu down wearily. "Look, we left things on bad terms, but—"

Just then his eyes slid and his face broke into a grin. "Candy!"

Convenient timing? She supposed she should be grateful for the interruption before things went down the same path as their last date.

Meet-up, she corrected herself.

"And Amelia!" Kyle's smile was positively wicked now.

Amelia stared at Brooke with wide eyes as she approached the table, while Candy simply clasped her hands and crooned, "Well, if that isn't the cutest couple to cross through that door all night!"

"Oh, we're just..." Brooke was momentarily at a loss for words. Finally, she said, "Catching up."

She caught Kyle's eye across the table and glanced away.

Amelia stared at her with plaintive interest, but Brooke knew her cousin wasn't the pushy or prying type. She'd wait for Brooke to come to her, to open up and share.

Candy, on the other hand...

"Oh? So you two know each other?" Recognition suddenly flashed in her eyes as she clasped a hand to her mouth. "Oh! Oh, you two were..."

"Married," Brooke said tightly. "Yes, Candy. Kyle and I are—I mean *were*—married." Her heart began to pound.

She caught his eye again and pinched her mouth against the mirth that positively shone in them.

"Well!" Candy seemed to be at a loss for words, and Amelia used the opportunity to point out that the pot pies might need to be removed from the oven.

Bless her.

"Shrimp and grits is the special tonight," Amelia said with a smile, once Candy had reluctantly walked away. "I promised when I took over the café that I would still keep some things the same."

Brooke nodded as she looked around the room, taking in the space and the changes that Amelia had implemented to make the business her own. "I love it. It still feels like the old café, but it's different. Improved."

She noticed that Kyle was frowning, all amusement seeming to have disappeared.

"I'll have the special," Brooke said quickly.

"Make that two," Kyle said. "And a bottle of Conway's best red."

Amelia glanced at Brooke as she collected the menus. "Coming right up."

"So, guess we're catching up then," Kyle said as he leaned into the table, grinning in triumph.

Brooke looked at the boy who had once held her hand and captured her heart, and she realized that she wasn't sure she wanted to know more about the Kyle that sat before her. It was easier to remember him as he was. A part of her past. And to tuck him away rather than dust him off.

"I'm afraid my life is rather dull. All work and no play as they say." She gave a small smile.

"New York wasn't everything you wanted it to be?"

She swallowed hard and sat a little straighter. "No, no, New York was great. Just…great. And I learned a ton, too. I'm very grateful for the experience."

He looked at her as if he didn't believe her, and why should he? Her tone was pitched and defensive and she wasn't even completely convinced. And she was back here, in Blue Harbor, less than six years after she had left.

Shame filled her, as it always did once the anger had cooled and she looked back on her part in their failed marriage.

Breaking his gaze, she looked around the room, smiling wistfully. "I remember coming here every Tuesday night for what must have been a year."

"Oh, it was more than that," Kyle said with a little smile.

"I remember that there used to be a painting on that wall, of the lighthouse out on Evening Island." She grinned as the memories came back to her. "And over in that corner, there was a photograph of the cook's dog, sitting in front of a bowl of spaghetti."

He laughed. "She loved that dog."

"And every Christmas there would be a jar of candy canes on the counter, and a long rope of tinsel with all the cards people had sent."

She felt warmer just thinking about it, back when life was simple and sure. When she knew what to expect when the day started. She'd taken that routine for granted. Craved excitement and change.

She frowned a little now.

"Is that all you remember?" Kyle tipped his head.

She thought about it. "Is there something I should remember?"

His eyes shadowed for a moment but he gave a tight smile. "I think you hit all the good parts."

She sighed. Things were different, but far from worse, and she was happy that her cousin had made the place her own. "The changes are nice, but it still feels the same." Still brought her back to another time and place. A happier time.

"The Conways always did have a good sense for business," Kyle observed. There was a pinch to his forehead that made Brooke wonder if there was more behind his words.

She considered asking, but she was too struck by what he said. Wishing too hard that it was true. Yes, most of the Conways had been successful in business. But would she?

They paused their conversation when their wine was delivered by a wide-eyed Candy, who had to press her lips together to keep from saying anything, it appeared.

Kyle said nothing as he filled their glasses. "My brother wants to make some changes to the pub," he finally said.

She looked at him in surprise, only that he would open up to her. There was no denying the fact that Harrison's was a dive bar. They made a decent burger and excellent fries, but it couldn't compete with the Carriage House, and from what she knew, that had never been the intention.

"I thought Ryan didn't care about the pub."

"He does now. Six years too late," Kyle said quietly.

*

By the time they'd finished the bottle of wine and had made their way through a meal that made Brooke want to shout out to all her city friends that when it came to comfort food, this café topped any New York eatery, Brooke was finally starting to relax.

"So you really don't miss it? The parties, the fashion shows? That was everything you ever wanted!"

Kyle was looking at her in wonder, not accusation, and she felt her edge soften.

Was it everything she ever wanted? Because there was one thing she'd wanted more. And that was him.

Maybe it was the wine, but she felt a prickle of tears touch the back of her eyes and she pushed them away before he could see. She brushed a brave hand through the air. "It was time. I learned, I experienced, and…Well, I'm not sure I ever would have found everything I was looking for in New York."

"And what's that?" he asked, his eyes soft and searching.

She felt her chest rise and fall with each breath until she managed to break his stare. "Oh, you know, family, my own shop. Rent in Manhattan is a fortune!" She smiled as if making a joke, but Kyle wasn't laughing. If anything, he looked as resigned as she felt.

Suddenly, Kyle leaned into the table, his elbows splayed, his face so close to her that she felt the urge to pull back, but she didn't.

"Just so you know," he whispered.

His blue eyes danced, and she stared at him, taking him in, even though so much of him was committed to memory. There was the bump on his nose that had appeared in the seventh grade without explanation, and the scar on his hand from his first mishap in shop class—he'd come a long way.

"Yes?" she asked a little breathlessly.

He licked his bottom lip, his grin quirking. "Candy's been over at the counter for the last ten minutes doing a really poor job of pretending to scrub it down."

Brooke felt the air escape her lungs. She managed a laugh, a nervous one. She wasn't sure what she'd been expecting Kyle to confide, but a distinct feeling of disappointment took hold, and it doubled when he leaned back against his chair, creating more space between them again.

Perhaps catching his eye, Candy hurried over to the table, her eyes darting eagerly from Brooke to Kyle and back again. "Dessert? Now, I didn't make it tonight, but it is still delicious. Berry crumble, with the first picking from the orchard, Brooke!" She grinned broadly and added, dropping her voice by a level, "But if you don't mind me saying, you two might want to come back on a Thursday. That's when I'm in charge of dessert, and oh, I make a caramel cheesecake that will make your eyes roll back into your heads."

Brooke laughed, almost happy for the interruption. Wait, what was she saying? Of course she was happy for the interruption! Being alone with Kyle Harrison was the last thing she needed right now.

Or wanted.

She swallowed hard.

"No wonder Uncle Dennis is marrying you," she chided.

But Candy just stood a little straighter and shook her head. "Oh, no. I mean, it helps and all, and he loves my skillet breakfasts. But he loves what comes before them more, if you follow."

Now it was Kyle's turn to sputter on his drink. Candy, however, winked and said, "I don't want to…interrupt. You two just holler if you want that dessert. I'll be right there at the counter."

Of course she would be.

Brooke stared at Kyle as Candy patted her on the shoulder and sauntered away. If there was any chance of prolonging this evening with a dessert course, that door had probably closed.

And it was better that way, Brooke told herself, as she pulled out her cardigan and shivered into the fabric.

"Well, this was…" She let her words hang there, not exactly knowing how to finish them. Fun? Not exactly? Nice? Maybe a little.

Confusing, she decided. It was very confusing.

"I'd offer to walk you home, but I can't be sure that Candy wouldn't be trailing us," Kyle whispered, and Brooke burst out laughing, loudly, too loudly, enough to probably catch Amelia's attention from the kitchen.

Enough to make something catch in Kyle's eye.

She felt her smile slip and something in her heart tug. Six years ago when they'd sat in this very restaurant, they never could have imagined that this was where they'd be today.

And that was why it was time to go home and clear her head, maybe do a little planning for tomorrow, think about her real life, the one she'd built for herself without Kyle.

9

Brooke could have put money on the fact that Candy would be her first customer of the day, and she wasn't the least surprised to see her future aunt push through the shop door within minutes of Brooke turning the sign in the window.

She held up a bakery bag and said, "I brought you a little breakfast. My specialty. No pressure."

Brooke wasn't so sure about that. Still, she took the bag and set it on her desk. "Thank you."

Candy eyed her quietly, her gaze darting back to the bag in a meaningful way.

Brooke politely lifted the bag again and looked inside to discover some small biscuits that were still warm and had the distinct aroma of cheddar.

"These smell delicious," she said, eliciting a beam from Candy.

"Just something I whipped up." When Brooke still didn't reach for one, Candy was sure to add, "They're actually my famous cheese biscuits. Amelia has them on the menu now, daily."

Brooke licked her bottom lip to hide her smile. What Candy lacked in modesty and discretion, she made up for in warmth, and Brooke could see how her uncle was revived by this woman. She was energetic, if a little eccentric, and she certainly added a welcome distraction to Brooke's morning.

Besides, she was getting used to seeing familiar faces, looked forward to it even.

Even when she shouldn't, she thought, pulling her thoughts from Kyle.

She grinned at Candy. "Well then, I don't see how I can resist."

It was a far cry from her usual breakfast of a poached egg with a single slice of toast, or a piece of fruit sliced onto yogurt. Still, when she took a bite, under Candy's scrutiny, she knew that she'd better not make a habit of letting Candy stop by at this hour. These were too good to resist.

"I can see why Amelia hired you!" She polished off one of the biscuits while Candy smiled gaily.

"It was only supposed to be temporary, but then, so was my contract with Denny!" Candy honked in laughter, and despite herself, Brooke joined in.

It was just what she needed—well, other than the extra calories—to get her mind off Kyle and onto lighter, easier thoughts. Still, as Candy continued to watch her carefully, she had the uneasy sensation that the woman was waiting for an opportunity to bring up Brooke's so-called date last night.

Instead, Brooke focused on Candy, not just because she was marrying into the family, but because it might help her have a better sense of direction for the wedding dress design and what kind of day Candy pictured.

"I heard about my uncle's fall last year," Brooke said, recalling the slip off the ladder that had resulted in two broken bones, and a caregiver who offered more than anyone had expected.

"At the orchard." Candy clucked. "He's fine now, thanks to a little tender loving care." She waggled her eyebrows. "But I think it's for the best that Britt took over the place. Plus, it leaves more time for Denny and me to…get to know each other better."

Oh, boy.

"I wondered how my uncle would manage when my father retired," Brooke said on a sigh. "None of us were ever quite as attached to the orchard as my cousins. Britt is definitely the best person to take it over, and I hear that she's doing a fine job."

"With the help of Robbie Bradford, of course. If Denny hadn't fallen off the ladder, I'm not sure Britt would have come back. And if she hadn't come back, she wouldn't have been reunited with her first love. It's funny how sometimes one event can alter the course of so many things."

Brooke raised her eyebrows. "I couldn't agree more. If I hadn't lost my job, I doubt I ever would have moved back to Blue Harbor."

"And aren't you glad you did?" Candy looked at her hopefully, but Brooke knew better than to take the bait. Instead, she shifted the conversation back to her cousin. "Britt seems very happy running the orchard, and it was very clever of my uncle to hire Robbie…"

Candy laughed. "Oh, no, he's not the matchmaker in the family. He's too practical for that sort of thing. Besides, I think he'd given up all hope of Britt moving back before his fall. No, I can't say that dear Denny is responsible for getting those two back together. I think it's just good old-fashioned fate."

"Fate?" Brooke was sure she looked as skeptical as she felt.

"Oh, I'm sure you hear that word a lot in here," Candy said, brushing a hand in the air. Her gaze, however, had turned up a notch in its intensity. "When two people are meant to be together, they find a way."

Brooke pulled in a breath. Sure enough. Though Amelia wasn't one to gossip, Brooke would bet money on the fact that Candy had managed to get the bare-bone facts out of her before the door of the café was locked last night.

"Robbie and Britt were meant to be. They went their different ways and life brought them back together. Older. Wiser." Candy looked around the empty shop in case anyone might overhear, and stage whispered, "If you ask me, it won't be too long before you have another dress to design."

"Fine by me!" Brooke was happy for her cousin. She and Robbie had been high school sweethearts, and even though life had taken them in different directions, it had also led them both back to Blue Harbor. And each other.

Her stomach shifted uneasily. Not that the same could be said for her and Kyle. No, their problems ran too deep.

"Love is funny," Candy said airily as she walked over to a rack of dresses, flinging a pointed look over her shoulder.

Brooke took her time rolling up the bakery bag. She'd save the rest for later. Maybe freeze them for another day when she needed a little pick me up.

"How so?" she asked, refusing to feed into Candy's obvious suggestion.

"Oh, you know, sometimes things have a way of working out when you least expect it." She paused, and perhaps sensing that Brooke's pleasant, neutral expression wasn't going to crack, continued, "I mean, look at me and Denny. I had been dating a man whose favorite past time was spitting cherry pits clear across the kitchen. I'd all but given up on the notion of romance! And then this man falls off a ladder, and his daughter calls for someone to tend to him for a bit. And I opened the door, and I just knew that everything was about to change. But only because I was willing to let it."

Brooke took a measured breath. "Yes, and sometimes it doesn't."

Candy's eyes burst open. "Don't say that too loudly, dear. It's bad for business." She marched over and squeezed Brooke's hand, giving her a look of concern. "Still nursing that broken heart over your marriage? You and Kyle Harrison seemed to be getting along just fine from what I could tell."

Brooke nodded. "It's a small town. There's no room for bad feelings."

Candy opened her mouth to protest, but Brooke quickly said, "Did you have any more thoughts on your dress? I haven't quite finished the sketches, but I can run you through my preliminary designs?"

Candy's face fell, and something told Brooke it had less to do with not seeing the sketches and more to do with not getting a little gossip out of Brooke.

"Oh, no rush. You did just get back to town and I'm sure that there are a lot of people that you're busy…catching up with." She stared at Brooke brazenly.

"Oh, I've seen most by now," Brooke said airily. "It was so nice seeing what Amelia did with the café. And the bakery! You must be so proud of Maddie."

She tipped her head, smiling pleasantly, watching as Candy struggled not to push things back onto her dinner with Kyle last night.

Eventually, she seemed to give up, thankfully.

"Well, speaking of the café, I need to get back," she said, looking so disappointed that Brooke almost felt bad for her. "I thought I'd…pop by for a minute. Get to know my future niece a bit more. We didn't have much time to talk last night."

Brooke smiled to show her appreciation. "Well, this was lovely. I'm always happy to have a visitor, especially one who brings me breakfast." She made a point of picking up her agenda and clicking her pen. "Did you want to make an appointment to look over those sketches?"

Again, frustration swept Candy's expression. "Whenever, dear. Amelia is always supportive for me to take a break or two throughout the day."

Brooke hid her smile and set down the book. "Let's check in next week."

Candy's eyes seemed to sparkle again. "It is exciting, getting married. But then, you already know that."

Oh, for crying out loud. Rather than be annoyed, Brooke was amused. Candy would soon learn that there was no story to be had here. That she and Kyle were just a thing of the past, and the most salacious thing about them was that they were technically still married.

Technically.

*

By the close of the day, Brooke could think of nothing but a hot bath and a cold glass of wine. It had been another good day, at least for the business, and she knew that she should focus on that rather than worry about anything that might go wrong. Design, like anything creative, was subjective. She couldn't take someone else's opinion personally, even though, when it came to people like her previous boss, that often felt impossible.

After Candy had left, most disappointed, and only after she had finally admitted defeat about dragging any good gossip from Brooke's lips, there had been three drop-ins, one follow-up consultation made, and a good meeting with the bride from Pine Falls, who was thrilled with the bridesmaid dress sketches. They'd narrowed it down to two designs, and Brooke decided to use the few remaining minutes of her workday selecting fabric samples from her back room. The space was small enough that if anyone came in, she'd hear the door jangle its bells.

She sighed happily when she flicked on the light in her fabric closet, where bolts of fabric were arranged by color and texture. The bride wanted her bridesmaids in blue, and Brooke had a very specific chiffon in mind—something that was soft, but not too literal. A shade that tended toward grey in certain lighting, and wouldn't compete with the bride. Something that would look gorgeous with the lake shimmering in the backdrop of the photos that would no doubt rest in frames for the next fifty years.

Or, in her case, more like fifty days.

She pulled in a sharp breath. She should have expected this. New York had been full of distraction. Every day brought a new face, and as the years passed by and her new life became less new and more regular, thoughts of Kyle faded into the past.

Which was where they belonged. The only reason that she was even thinking about him now was because of all these ridiculous dates he insisted upon. She had plenty to occupy her mind, after all. This boutique being the primary one.

She consulted the swatches again, deciding to add one more to the mix in a deeper shade, closer to navy. Of course, the fabric she wanted was on the very top shelf, and even standing on her tiptoes, she couldn't reach it. Still, her step stool was upstairs in her apartment; she'd been using it to dust the tops of her kitchen cabinets last night when she couldn't fall asleep, and she didn't want to leave the shop unattended at all, not even to dash up the back stairs. She tried again, shifting a few bolts around, and then, before she could even process what was happening, shrieked as all the shelves seemed to collapse on each other and the fabric came tumbling down around her.

From behind her, she heard the husky rumble of a laugh, and she darted her eyes over her shoulder to see none other than Kyle standing in the open doorway, taking in the sight.

"Looks like I arrived just in time," he said with a rather cocky grin.

She glared at him. "More like you distracted me."

"Distracted you? But you didn't even seem to hear me come in."

That was true, all true, but so was what she had said. He was on her mind, day and night, and she wasn't thinking clearly.

"Here, let me help you," he said, reaching out a hand to help her up.

She wanted to snatch her arm away, but she was wearing those ridiculous stiletto strappy sandals that she'd always known would be the death of her one day, and so, with gritted teeth, she held out a hand.

He took it. And oh, it felt good. Warm and familiar and as comforting as her favorite old blanket, and she wasn't so sure if that was a good or a bad thing. Only as he hoisted her to her feet, and she steadied herself on her heels, their eyes locked and she knew that it was a bad thing. Very bad. His eyes were locked on hers, as if he was searching for something, or waiting for something. And his hand, it still held hers, and to her horror, she realized that she wasn't a passive recipient here. She was holding his hand back, long after she needed assistance.

Quickly, she pulled herself free and turned, looking at the bolts that had now fallen to the floor. She could forget the bath and wine, at least for a few hours. This fabric was nearly as important as the gowns themselves. She could already see wrinkles appearing on the taffeta; she'd have to steam it carefully before she restocked it.

And there would be no restocking until she had fixed the shelves.

She checked her watch. It was past five now. She doubted that Gus would be willing to come by on such short notice, and her father was many things, but handy had never been at the top of the list for the Conway brothers. Her uncle Dennis had fallen off a ladder last year, after all!

"I should call Gus and see if he can get over here soon," she said. Or maybe Cole McCarthy—pull in the old family favor now that he was dating her cousin Maddie. He was a fine contractor; the bakery was proof of that.

"I can get these shelves back up for you," Kyle said simply, not that she'd be hinting, or wanting that. No, what she wanted was for Kyle to have never come inside. For him to drop this stupid agreement.

What she wanted was to never see him again. To forget him.

Easier said than done, she thought.

He inspected the wall, and then looked down at the shelves. "These are old. And you did have them stuffed to capacity."

"I like fabric," she said simply.

His mouth lifted. "I think that's obvious. But then, you always did."

She grinned, remembering their last Christmas together when all she'd asked for was three yards of embroidered linen to make the curtains for the cottage they'd already planned to move into. Kyle had assumed she was joking, but she wasn't, and when he saw the delight in her face when she opened the box, he'd seen firsthand how much this meant to her. Designing. Creating.

It was the last time she truly felt he had supported her dreams.

"Fine." She blew out a sigh. Fixing her shelves was the least he could do for her, all things considered. "And thank you," she added, more than a little begrudgingly.

Still, it was nice of him, and she knew that Gus rarely took on small projects. She'd been lucky to get him over to hang some lights and the sign out front. Fixing shelves would hardly classify as an emergency to him, even if those shelves did hold some of her most cherished possessions.

She began to carefully gather up the fabric and prop the boards against the wall.

"Do you have a toolbox around here?" Kyle asked.

"No, actually." She wondered if the hardware store was still open, and assumed that it was. Would they go together? That would certainly get half the town talking.

"I've got one back at the pub," Kyle offered. He scrutinized the shelves as Brooke cleared away the fabric. "This is going to take a while. I can bring back something for dinner if you're hungry?"

At the mention of food, Brooke's stomach grumbled loud enough for Kyle to hear. His eyebrows shot up before he burst out laughing. Brooke's cheeks flamed with heat.

"I'll take that as a yes."

"Only because I'm hungry," she told him. As if that much wasn't obvious. Still, she didn't want him to think this was anything more. Unless... "Although it could count toward part of our agreement. If we're spending the evening together, and food is involved."

Kyle's laughter stopped when he gave her a long, unreadable look. "I'll be back in a bit."

Brooke watched him go without a word, feeling sad at how she'd ruined a moment and even sadder that she could no longer read his expressions. Once there had been a time when she knew Kyle as well as she knew her sisters. She could tell when he was happy, excited, sad, mad, all without him even opening his mouth. She could anticipate his every move, and now, he seemed unpredictable. Did he really want to spend his evening fixing her broken shelves?

And if he did, then why?

10

Brooke couldn't afford to think about Kyle right now. As she stood, worrying over her soon-to-be ex-husband, her fabric was getting wrinkled and in danger of being stepped on, and given how much of her savings she'd already sunk into the business, she didn't exactly have the funds to replace anything, and even if she did, she was thousands of miles from Manhattan, and she highly doubted the craft store in the neighboring town of Pine Falls carried anything she could use.

She did her best, stacking bolts of lace and satin on her desk, the coffee table in the seating area, and on the velvet benches in the dressing rooms. By the time she was finished, Kyle was back, holding a toolbox in one hand and a pizza box in the other. He shook some water from his hair.

"Storm's rolling in," he said.

Spring showers, she thought, remembering how much she loved the smell of rain at this time of year, how it made the grass greener, the flowers bigger, and always gave her the best night's sleep.

She eyed the pizza box from Fiorre's—the place she only ever went with Kyle. Her family was more of a Martino's supporter because the Martino family lived two doors down, and Mrs. Martino and Brooke's mother were in the same bridge club. But Fiorre's was the best pizza in town. Maybe the best in the Midwest. It certainly gave some of the New York joints a bit of competition. The smell was enough to make her mouth water, and she didn't have to look to know the toppings he'd selected.

"House special?" she asked, eyeing the box greedily.

"Is there any other choice?" He gave a little grin. It was their usual order.

"Hawaiian, if you ask one of my sisters," she laughed.

"It's still hot," he said, giving her a look that she did recognize. It was an invitation.

Despite her reservations, she wasn't about to pass up a steaming hot slice of pizza covered in all her favorite toppings. She looked around the storefront, at the pristine dresses in various shades of white and ivory and her fabric, which was piled neatly on every available surface other than the floor.

Her eyes darted outside, hoping they could sit on a bench, perhaps, but the rain showed no signs of slowing.

"I guess we should take this upstairs." As soon as she caught the look on his face, she added, "I don't allow food in the shop."

"And here I thought you actually wanted to invite me in," he bantered.

But she had done just that, hadn't she? She'd opened the door to him, even when she'd been so clear she was determined to shut it.

She looked at the man before her. The years had been good to him. Filled out his frame and gave a weathered look to his already kind eyes. It was the eyes that pulled her in, brought her back to a time and place when she felt whole, and content. Kyle had always been easygoing, thoughtful, and loyal. She'd had as much fun at his side as she did with her sisters, and that was saying a lot, considering she and Gabby and Jenna rarely argued. He was good for laughs, up for a night out as much as a night in, great at telling stories, good at listening, too. She'd never stopped liking him, she realized. And that was just the problem.

"Seriously, the last thing I need is grease on my fabric." Resigned to the fact that she had no other choice, she led him and the pizza to the back of the shop and opened the door to the stairwell.

She eyed him as she held it open for him to pass. No, she thought, grease on her fabric wasn't the last thing she needed. The absolute last thing she needed was to be spending yet another evening with Kyle.

And enjoying it more than she should.

*

Kyle didn't know what to make of Brooke's apartment. He noted the small bunch of flowers sitting in a vase on the counter, the blanket tossed over the old sofa, and a glimpse of some framed photos on the bedside table through the half-open door.

It was a nice space, with big windows looking over Main Street, and tidy, sparse furnishings, with small touches that showed she had already made herself at home.

RETURN TO ME

Maybe that was what didn't sit right. Brooke's home should be the cottage tucked at the end of a gravel road, the one with the dining table he'd carved for her, the one with the curtains she'd sewn hanging from the windows, and the two chairs he'd made sitting side by side out on the water's edge. The place they'd chosen and shared.

The place where he still lived.

Now, the reality that she had moved on hit him harder than it did when she'd gone to New York. It was impossible to picture her life there, to a place he'd only been once, for Christmas, as a kid. He imagined heavy traffic and loud sirens and a cramped apartment. He'd dared to think that she was unhappy. That she'd come to her senses. Return to Blue Harbor.

And she had. Only not for him.

And now, she had her own place, here in their town. She had her own furniture, limited as it may be, and photos in frames of events he wasn't part of, and a fridge full of food that was only for her. She'd an entire new life for herself.

While he'd stayed behind, letting the years pass, clinging to the past. Maybe too much of the past.

He couldn't deny the irony of it. It was exactly what she'd accused him of doing, after all. Not changing. Not thinking of the future. Was it so bad that he liked things just as they were and had always been?

Given that she'd left him, he supposed it was.

"Something to drink?" Brooke was looking at him expectantly, and he forced his attention back to the present.

"Afraid I don't buy beer, but I have wine. Family blend, of course."

"Of course." His smile felt tight. "I'll take a glass. Don't worry. I promise your shelves won't come out crooked."

"You can handle your own," she said wryly. "Besides, you're a better carpenter than Gus and Cole combined."

He knew that she wasn't just flattering him, and the compliment was one he didn't quite know how to take. Once, working with his hands, sanding and chiseling until he had created something he could be proud of was part of his daily life. It had been a long time since anyone asked about his woodwork. Most people in town probably forgot about it by now, even his mother barely mentioned it, probably because she suspected it was a sore spot for him, much the way she never mentioned Brooke either.

But then, Brooke hadn't witnessed the lapse of time these past years. She just remembered where they left off. Back when he was still dreaming big, sketching designs. Married to her in every meaning of the word.

Looking around the room, he supposed he could say he was guilty of the same. He wanted Brooke to be that girl so full of ideas and hope and excitement for life. So full of love for him. But time had gone by, slowly at first, and then steadily, and yesterday was a very long time ago.

Instead, he saw someone who was a little more withdrawn, a little more uptight, and a little less happy.

He frowned when he considered his part in all of that.

Brooke opened a cabinet and pulled out two wine glasses, then a drawer to retrieve a corkscrew. It was amazing that something so innocent could feel like a stab to his chest.

This was her world. And he had no place in it.

There was no table, two mismatched sofas, and a coffee table made of glass. It suddenly felt awkward to be here, in her space, a guest in his wife's house, forcing something that was done and over with years ago, even though that's what he'd been trying to do these last few days. But it was different when they were on neutral territory.

He was relieved when Brooke tipped her chin toward the hallway. "I have a balcony out back. It's covered, so we shouldn't get too wet. I've been cooped up all day," she added, in case further explanation was needed.

It wasn't.

"That sounds great," he said, grabbing the pizza in one hand and the bottle of wine in the other.

Soon, they were seated at a small wrought-iron table that Brooke explained had come with the apartment.

"Nice perk," he said gamely. It was better being outside, away from all of her new things, even though some, or most, weren't very new at all, just new to him.

Brooke bit into a slice of pizza. He was happy to see that New York hadn't rubbed off on her too much. No folding of the crust was taking place. She was still eating it straight-on, like the Midwestern girl he knew.

And loved.

He swallowed hard, thinking of how familiar this was, even when it was strange at the same time. He didn't know where she kept her corkscrew or what cabinet held her glasses. He didn't know how she'd spent every day and night of the past six years, or what her New York apartment had looked like. But he knew her past. He knew her story. And he knew her heart.

Or at least he had. Once.

He tore his gaze from her profile. Grabbed a slice and took a big bite. Drowned his sorrows with a big gulp of wine after that, even if he did prefer beer.

"This is a nice apartment," he said.

"It's convenient, but it doesn't feel like home yet." She eyed him. "How about you…Are you still…"

"I'm still at the cottage."

A look of mild surprise took over her face, but she composed herself quickly. "I keep meaning to personalize the apartment more, but the business is taking up a lot of my time."

"So you think you'll stay then?"

"In the apartment?" She gave him a smile that seemed almost apologetic. "It needs some more furniture, but that's the plan."

"You always liked a plan," he said, and even though he meant it with nostalgia, there was an edge of resentment to his tone that he was sure she had noticed.

"It's easier for me to plan than float along. Life passes by otherwise. I didn't want it to pass me by."

"Oh, now, I don't think that would have ever happened." He gave her a resigned smile that she met in return. "But you don't miss New York yet?"

He still couldn't believe it. Brooke, who couldn't wait to get out of Blue Harbor and make a name for herself, had come back to their small town only years later. Maybe the part he couldn't accept was that she hadn't come back for him.

Brooke sighed heavily and filled her glass with wine. "It was great, don't get me wrong," she was sure to add, lest he dared to hope that she had been nothing short of miserable and regretful about her decision to move there, "but I'm older now, and I have the experience I need, and I was never going to be able to break out on my own there, not really."

"You so sure about that?"

She didn't look sure, and her sigh was heavy before she spoke. "It was a tough business. Long hours and not a lot of upward mobility. My boss and I had a lot of creative differences. Maybe…"

She stopped to take a bite of her pizza as if she wasn't sure she wanted to continue. "Maybe I didn't have what it took."

She shrugged, managed a tight smile, but he could see the hurt in her eyes.

"Impossible," he said, giving her his best grin until he pulled a smile out of her. "I saw your dresses in the shop. That's true talent right there. Don't let one person's opinion make you doubt yourself."

"Sometimes one person's opinion matters the most," she said quietly. She looked away, clearing her throat. "Thank you for saying that. It means a lot."

They sat in silence for a moment, looking out onto the rain hitting the grass below, and he thought of what to say next, but came up blank. After she'd first left, there had been a hundred things he wanted to say to her, and some that he'd wished he had. Don't go, being at the top of the list. Or, wait for me. Eventually, it shifted to, Come back to me. But there was anger in there, too, mixed with understanding. He'd made a choice. She'd responded to it. And he'd had to live with the outcome.

Now, all that seemed like a very long time ago, and with her back in town, most of it felt pointless.

"Everyone gets stuck with a bad boss at some point." He started to laugh when he remembered one of her complaints from years back. "Remember how Patsy had said you weren't pushy enough? How she wanted you to up-sell the customers? Tell them they needed accessories?"

Brooke covered her mouth, laughing. "Oh, I forgot about that! She used to have me push the most expensive items, too. If the red blouse had the biggest price tag, then everyone who came in the shop that day had to be told that red was their color." She shook her head. "I'm surprised you remembered that."

His laughter faded. "That's the funny part about sharing a life with someone. Your memories are shared too."

She nodded, and then set her pizza down, her smile waning. "Patsy was hardly the ideal boss, but I did learn a lot about retail from her, and when Gabby told me she was closing her store...it felt like a sign."

He frowned at her. "A sign? I thought you didn't believe in those things."

The girl he knew would scoff if he suggested they get their palms read at the county fair or roll her eyes when her sister read the horoscope pages. Brooke was exactly what she said she was: a planner. She made choices; she didn't let life happen. She took it by the reins, and heck if he didn't admire her for it, even if it had eventually led her away from him.

"Well, I don't believe in fate and superstition and all. I believe in hard work. But I also believe in opportunity. I guess I saw this as an opportunity. It made my decision very easy. I hadn't been actively thinking of returning until I heard about the space, and then...Well, it was like the idea was planted, and the decision was made."

"If I'd known it was that easy to get you back here, I would have driven Patsy out of business years ago," Kyle only half joked.

Brooke sipped her wine. There was tension in her eyes. "Or you could have just driven to New York."

Now it was his turn to feel tense. "You know I couldn't do that," he said quietly.

"Couldn't or wouldn't?" She shook her head. "Forget it. There's no sense in rehashing it. What's done is done."

Kyle felt his pulse quicken. "Well, it's not over yet. You're still my wife."

She sighed heavily. "Only because we haven't filed the paperwork yet, Kyle."

"And why haven't we?" He knew why he hadn't, and with each day and then month and then year that went by, he'd dared to think she felt the same. That somehow, someday, they'd find a way back to each other.

That hope had made the long days shorter. Made the nights a little less lonely.

She blinked at him. "Because there was no reason to before."

He nodded. He supposed it was true. Neither of them had moved on romantically, work had remained a top priority for both of them. And now, Brooke needed to qualify for a loan.

They both did, he thought, recalling his recent conversations with his brother about the state of the pub.

"About Harrison's—" he started, but she held up a hand.

"Kyle, we both did what we needed to do. I was angry and hurt, but I also know that you didn't do anything to actively upset me. I know how much you cared about your dad," she added gently.

He swallowed hard, knowing that was only the half-truth. "But I cared about you too, Brooke."

And he still did.

He stared at her, at the face he knew so well, even if there was so much about her that was new and foreign to him. Underneath it all, she was the same person that he'd fallen in love with and never stopped.

She looked at him, blinking slowly, and the only sound that he could hear was the rain falling slowly and steadily. He felt a pull, drawing him closer to her, wanting to kiss her, to go back to that time and place where everything was just as it was supposed to be, when she was his and the future was theirs.

She stiffened and quickly began gathering up the pizza box. "The wind's picking up. We won't stay dry out here much longer."

Sure, the rain was starting to blow onto the balcony, but Kyle wouldn't have minded getting a little wet.

"We had our first kiss in the rain," he reminded her. "You didn't mind getting your hair a little wet then."

Her hands stilled on the pizza box for a moment but then she stood, saying briskly, "Well, I didn't have expensive highlights back then."

He arched a brow. Used the opportunity as an excuse to let himself properly stare at her, take her all in. "Is that what's different about you?"

Her smile was gone now. "A lot's different about me, Kyle."

Yes, he realized with a heaviness in his chest. A lot was different. Her smile was gone, and so was her lightness, her carefree laughter, and maybe even some of her optimism.

And maybe he was to blame for that.

"Well," he said, clearing his throat. "I should probably get started on those shelves."

"It's fine. I'll call Gus in the morning. Really."

But Kyle shook his head. "I'm a man of my word," he said, with a little grin, but there was a sadness that came over Brooke's eyes.

"Yes, you are," she said.

And they both knew that she was referring to his insistence to take over the pub after his father's passing, even if it had cost him everything else that mattered.

Especially her.

11

By Friday night, Brooke was almost surprised that Kyle hadn't tried to tie her down with another date, not that she didn't have an excuse handy. It was ladies night, or at least that's what Gabby was calling it. Her sister was determined to make up for lost time.

She wasn't the only one, Brooke thought wryly.

Brooke sat at her desk in the shop, putting the finishing touches on the bridesmaid dress sketches for her Pine Falls client until her alarm clock alerted her that it was time to go. She smiled to herself. Yes, she was a planner, but she was also the type to get lost in a creative endeavor and lose all touch with time and the outside world, and if there was one thing Brooke didn't like, it was showing up late.

Or letting people down.

She swallowed back the bitter taste when she considered that Kyle hadn't felt the same compulsion. He'd let her down in more ways than one, and he hadn't apologized for it yet either.

Maybe it was because he was content with his choice. No regrets.

Whereas she…

Brooke shook that off. Three meet-ups down, three to go. She didn't know why the thought depressed her. She was only halfway through her time with Kyle, and so far, all it had accomplished was making her think more about the past than she'd cared to ever before.

With a light denim jacket draped over her arm, she locked up behind her and hurried down the street toward the Yacht Club, tonight's rendezvous of choice, not that she was arguing. No Bradfords. No Harrisons. With any luck, none of the guys in their life at all. A proper ladies night *was* in order. She didn't even want to talk about men.

Unfortunately, Gabby had other ideas.

"See the guy over at the bar?" she asked, jutting her chin. "I caught his eye and smiled at him only to watch his wife appear thirty seconds later and plant a kiss on his mouth."

Brooke laughed and pulled out her chair. "I thought this was a ladies night."

Gabby groaned. "I know, but I need to get my mind off Candy." She poured Brooke a margarita from the pitcher she'd already ordered.

"Uh-oh, what happened?" She tried not to laugh. Chances were, in due time, she'd be having issues of her own with the blushing bride-to-be.

"Oh, more new ideas for the flowers, of course. Every week it's something. I don't know how many times I'm supposed to redesign it all!"

Brooke bit her lip. That was an issue.

She took a sip of her drink and thought about it. "Maybe we can join forces. Put some rules in place? I want to keep my clients happy, but I also can't come up with fifteen different designs and then have more and more changes."

"A fixed number of revisions before an hourly rate starts to apply?" Gabby laughed but then shrugged. "I hate to say it, but it might be necessary for some of the more demanding customers."

"It's one more aspect of running a business that I hadn't considered until now." Brooke sighed.

Gabby frowned at her. "Hey, you're where you're supposed to be. Doing what you love."

Brooke chewed her lip. The doubts were there, still, and she didn't want to get into it, not when just thinking about how her time had been spent in New York made her feel uneasy. Had she honed her skills, learned tricks of the trade that would make her more of a success here than she ever would have been in the city?

Or had she thrown everything away, only to end up not having what it took? Just to end up back in her hometown, right where she'd started?

"Speaking of love," Gabby said, and despite herself, Brooke had to laugh. "Hey, I can't help it! I wrote the sweetest card today for a husband who wanted to surprise his wife on their fiftieth wedding anniversary with fifty long-stem roses. Fifty years together! Can you even imagine?"

Brooke pulled in a breath and leveled her sister with a look. No, she clearly couldn't imagine. She and Kyle hadn't even lasted fifty days.

"Fifty years and I can't even remember the last time I was on a date, can you?"

Brooke paused, wondering if the other night with Kyle counted. No, she told herself firmly. Absolutely not. She was fulfilling a promise.

More like an obligation.

"I didn't date much in New York," Brooke said. "I was too focused on my career."

Her boss's words echoed back to her. Too ambitious. Was it true? Had she given up everything for the sake of her aspirations?

And everyone?

She forced a playful smile. "Besides, who needs a date when you can have a pitcher of margaritas with me?"

Gabby pouted dramatically. "Before I forget, Mom wants us to all come over next Sunday. Just something casual. Pizza. You in?"

Brooke was surprised that her sister would even ask such a thing. "Of course! I was thinking of stopping by tomorrow but maybe I'll hold off, catch up on work."

"You can't work too late tomorrow," Gabby warned. "It's the Blossom Barn Dance!"

The Blossom Barn Dance. It was common knowledge that the town event was taking place this weekend, but Brooke had been away too long to think about these things.

"I suppose I should go." She'd make an appearance after she closed her shop.

"Um, you sort of have to. You're a Conway, and there's no excuse now that you're back in town. I hope you won't forget next Sunday's dinner, too."

"Of course not!" Brooke said, hearing a defensive edge in her tone. "I don't want to miss out on any more than I already have."

"Good. Family dinners haven't been the same without you, though I have a feeling that New York has far better pizza."

"But not better company." Brooke grinned, but her stomach rolled over at the thought of the last time she'd shared a pizza, and with whom. How it had been so much better than any slice that she'd eaten in New York, and she couldn't necessarily say that it was on account of taste.

Gabby faked a swoon. "Is your shop open tomorrow?"

"Why? Are you in the market for a wedding dress?" Brooke joked.

Gabby gave an exaggerated pout. "It's starting to feel like I never will be."

Brooke gave her sister a sympathetic smile. "Would that be the worst thing in the world?"

"Maybe it's old fashioned of me, but I do want to find true love."

"Not every ending is a happy one," Brooke warned.

Gabby's eyes flashed. "I hope you don't go telling your customers that."

Brooke laughed but realized she should probably keep her personal feelings under tighter control. "I'm just saying, as your sister, that I've been married. And I've been alone for the past six years, too. And I'm not unhappy."

"Not unhappy isn't the same as happy," Gabby pointed out. She narrowed her gaze on Brooke. "Are you saying you were happier being married?"

"No!" Brooke was affronted. "I left Kyle, as you may recall," she whispered, looking around. Really, though, it hadn't felt like that. She may have been the one going, but he was the one who bailed on their plans. On their life together.

"I know! The whole town knows. I was wondering if I detected a hint of regret, that's all."

"Absolutely not!" But even as she said it, Brooke could felt a tightening in her stomach that made her wonder if her sister had managed to tap into the truth. She had a routine in New York—going to shows, putting in long hours, and barely having much time in her apartment before the day started all over again. She didn't have time to miss Kyle or think about what she was missing, or what she'd given up. Now, being back in town, spending time with him again, well, it was only natural that she might start to wonder...

She shook that thought right out of her head. Nonsense. She was rewriting history, or at best, ignoring it.

"Kyle and I didn't want the same things," she reminded Gabby.

"To live in this town?" Gabby had homed in on the main issue. "But now you're back. That doesn't make you wonder how things might have turned out if you had never left?"

"I had to leave," Brooke said firmly. She could hear the insistence in her tone and she knew that her sister was aware of it, too. She was trying to convince herself. Or remind herself. "I wouldn't be where I am today if I'd stayed. And if I'd stayed, then I would have been wondering what if I'd left, every day of my life. I would have resented Kyle. The ending still would have been the same."

"Unhappy," Gabby said matter-of-factly. She sighed. "What can I say? I like a happy ending."

"Well, my story isn't over just yet," Brooke said, relieved to be off the subject of Kyle Harrison. "And yours hasn't even started. Is there really *no one* in town you have your eye on?"

Gabby scoffed. "Please."

For someone as desperate to find true love as Gabby had always been, she was also willing to hold out for the right guy.

Something that Brooke should have done, maybe, except Kyle had always felt right.

And something about him still did.

*

The pub was always busy on Friday nights, and seeing that Kyle had cut his shift short last week to meet Brooke, he saw no way of skipping out early tonight. It was okay though. He'd seen Brooke three times in the past week—meaning he was halfway through their arranged time together. He needed to slow down, think things through before the next three dates slipped away.

Dates. He knew that's not what they were, but last night, and even at the café, it had felt like that. Like old times, almost.

And that was what he had wanted, wasn't it?

Yes, he thought. Still stuck in the past. Still trying to go back to some place and time. Still maybe trying to have it all.

Kyle checked on the cook in the kitchen, knowing that sometimes a special had to be scratched from the board, and even though everything was running smoothly, he couldn't fight off the frown when he pushed into the front room and joined his brother behind the bar.

"And here I thought you might be happy to see me." Ryan had never been good at sensing the timing of a joke, and Kyle was in no mood.

"I have things on my mind," he said, refusing to feed into the banter as he swung a towel over a shoulder and took an order from the two regulars at the end of the bar.

"That makes two of us," Ryan said, standing beside him. "We still have to talk about the budget. The forecast."

Kyle let go of the tap and shot his brother a scowl. "What are you, a weatherman now?"

"Very funny," Ryan said, even though all merriment had left his eyes. "You know I'm good with numbers, Kyle. And this place…this place isn't. It won't survive another year without some changes."

Kyle slid the two men their beers and turned to face Ryan, keeping his voice low. "I'm aware of that."

"Then what were you planning on doing about it?"

Kyle didn't answer that question. They both knew that Kyle had hoped things would turn around, just like he'd once hoped that Brooke would turn around. That things would all work out in the end. That he wouldn't have to make any dramatic changes to end up with what he'd always wanted.

And this pub, much as he had never wanted it, was important to him. He didn't want to lose it any more than he wanted to change it. And now his hand was being forced.

"Fine, we can discuss some changes," he said curtly. Seeing the raise of his brother's eyebrows, he added, "But not now. It's Friday night, and we're counting on this business. How else are we supposed to pay for these big ideas?"

"It will be difficult enough to qualify for a loan," Ryan said. "You ever think about selling the house? Might make you a better candidate if you had some cash in the bank."

Kyle grew quiet for a moment as he rinsed out glasses in the sink. The house had been a rental when he and Brooke took it, but they'd loved it, and after she was gone, it was the only piece of her that remained. When the time came for the owner to sell, Kyle had worked out a deal with him.

He said nothing, thinking that he should suggest they put the loan in his brother's name only. But that would mean giving his brother full control of the place. And he didn't trust him not to change it too much.

"Kyle Harrison!"

He turned to see Robbie and Matt Bradford drop onto stools at the center of the bar. Immediately, his spirits lifted. With the cousins here, the conversation would be light, his brother would get off his back for a bit, and he'd be reminded of all the reasons he'd held onto this place. Good company was as important to him as it had been to his father.

"Not out with the ladies tonight?" he asked. He caught the edge to his tone. It wasn't lost on him that both these men were reunited with Conway girls while Brooke was slipping further from his fingertips by the day.

"Amelia's at the café," Matt offered up, which of course Kyle knew. The Firefly Café was especially busy in the warmer months when patrons could sit on the deck overlooking Lake Huron.

"Keira's sleeping over at a friend's house, so I'm flying solo," Robbie said. He always smiled when he talked about his daughter. "It's sort of a strange feeling."

Kyle nodded. He knew all too well how empty life could feel, how long and lonely the evenings were, especially in those first few months after Brooke had left. He'd gotten used to it in time. Went out with the guys. Made sure to stay late at the pub, well past closing. Anything to delay returning to that quiet cottage.

But lately, the feeling had reared to the surface again, and all he could think of was how close Brooke was…and how far away at the same time.

"What about Britt?" he asked.

Robbie raised his eyebrows. "Oh, the orchard is sponsoring the school prom next weekend. I guess she got roped into helping with the decorating committee. Said they're lacking volunteers." He shook his head. "Prom. Feels like a hundred years ago, doesn't it?"

Kyle nodded, even though it felt more like yesterday. He could still remember the way Brooke had worn her hair that night, swept up into a low bun that she'd copied out of a magazine. Her nails had been painted the same shade of pink as her dress, and he'd picked out a matching corsage, all on his own, back when the flower shop was owned by a seemingly sweet older woman with a sharp eye and even sharper sense of business, who made sure to steer him toward the most expensive options, claiming that he wouldn't want to disappoint his lady, would he?

No, he thought now, with a heavy heart. He'd never set out to disappoint Brooke about anything, but somehow that's exactly what he'd done.

"Next weekend, you said?" He grinned to himself. He suddenly had the perfect way to spend their next date together.

12

Conway Orchard and Winery would always remain Brooke's favorite place in all of Blue Harbor—nearly as special as her childhood home, and even topping the lakefront, with its shimmering water and view of Evening Island.

When she was younger, she and her sisters and cousins would run through the orchard, playing hide and go seek until they'd reached the farm boundary, or helping their mothers to sell jams and pies. There were festivals and events, too, and this weekend was always Brooke's personal favorite. The Blossom Barn Dance was held every spring when the cherry trees were in full bloom. Somehow, like today, the sun always shone, and the rain stayed away, bringing everyone together at the orchard for a community gathering that lasted past sundown.

It was a time to laugh and sing and dance, and catch up with people you saw every day but didn't always have a chance to stop and talk with properly.

Tonight, though, she wasn't sure what she would share. The business. Yes, she'd keep focused on that. And helping her cousins.

RETURN TO ME

Spotting the line for Maddie's pies, she joined the end of it, hoping that her cousin wouldn't run out before Brooke's turn came.

"You're out of luck," Maddie said to her after she handed over a delicious strawberry pie with a sparkling sugary lattice crust to a young couple who were probably passing through town for the weekend. "That was my last pie, and after I clean up, I'm free to enjoy the music."

She smiled at something over Brooke's shoulder. More like someone, Brooke thought, noticing Cole standing near the band.

"I don't know where you find the time to make all of these and run the bakery," Brooke told her cousin. She had only been open for a week and a half and already she was struggling to think of when she could be able to finish the bridesmaid dress sketches for her Pine Falls client, much less start working on any new sample gowns.

"I have a great assistant who helps me in the kitchen," Maddie said. "And she's happy to cover Sunday mornings on her own so I can be here at the market too. I wouldn't want to miss it. Selling these pies is a family tradition."

Brooke smiled fondly at the memory of her Aunt Elizabeth standing in this very barn, selling her pies that looked exactly like Maddie's. She knew from experience that these pies would taste the same, too.

"There's something to be said for tradition," Brooke agreed. "It's something I think about with my wedding gowns. How they might get passed down through the generations."

"Speaking of wedding gowns, I heard that Candy already paid you a visit." Maddie waggled her eyebrows.

Brooke laughed. "That she did. She's certainly excited about the wedding."

"Is she wearing white?" Maddie wanted to know.

Brooke was aware that this was delicate territory. No one wanted to feel like their mother was being replaced, even if Candy couldn't be more different than Elizabeth Conway.

"Well, it is her first wedding," Brooke said carefully.

Maddie's cheeks flushed a bit but then she shrugged. "Honestly, I was worried her dress would be pink!"

Now they both laughed, and Brooke decided to keep it to herself that there was no doubt the bridesmaid gowns would be pink. She wondered as she walked around the barn if Candy might ask her to design those too and decided not to push her luck. She had plenty of business right now, and she didn't want to stretch herself too thin during her first few months. It was challenging enough to pour her savings into rent, let alone inventory costs. The loan would go a long way toward growth.

Leaving Maddie to close up her stand, Brooke wandered around the room, admiring the wildflower bouquets on the round tables.

Gabby motioned to her from the buffet table, which was piled with trays of food that Amelia had brought over from the café. Brooke noticed Candy's cheese biscuits and helped herself to one.

"No fresh faces." Gabby sighed and sipped her wine. "I suppose you can be my dance partner like when we were little."

"I can't stay long," Brooke admitted, knowing that the work she should be doing in her shop was not the only excuse. This was a town event, and chances were high that Kyle or at least his mother would stop by at some point.

"Come on! You've missed this while you were away!" Gabby chided.

It was true. She had. More than she'd admitted to herself.

"Fine, but if I fall behind on orders, I'm going to reinstate your sewing lessons." She laughed at Gabby's expression of horror because they both knew how that had gone. When they were still playing with dolls, Brooke had been the one to make their clothes, and despite her efforts, Gabby showed no effort or talent when it came to doing the same. She was an expert at flower crowns and necklaces though.

"If you're looking for an assistant, I heard that Heidi might need a job," she said, referring to their cousin on their mother's side. "She's never quite figured out what she wants to do, and this might be a good fit for you both. I'd hire her myself, but with mom helping with deliveries, I'm mostly covered."

Brooke couldn't deny that it was a tempting idea. Heidi was easygoing and creative, and a hard worker, too.

"She doesn't want to help her sister at the bookstore?"

Gabby gave a tight shake of the head. "That didn't work out."

"I'll need to wait to settle in," she told Gabby. "Once I know how much business I have, I'll be in a better position to make a long-term plan."

Gabby nodded, no explanation needed. But she grinned. "Long-term plan. I love the sound of that."

So did Brooke. Especially when it was one she could rely on.

The music turned to something catchy and Gabby gave her a pleading look. "I'll join you soon," Brooke promised.

She watched as her sister joined Jenna, her gaze roaming to Britt and Robbie who were sharing their dance with a little girl who must be Robbie's daughter, judging by the hair color and the way she giggled every time she looked up at him.

She smiled sadly, taking in the scene, thinking of how much had changed, and for so many people, herself included. It was hot in the room, mostly from the energy level, and she pushed her way through the crowd until she was outside in the cool evening air. It was quiet enough to hear the crickets chirping, and clear enough to see the stars, which were so much better than any city lights.

"Trade you for your thoughts."

Brooke turned at the sound of the low, deep voice, her breath catching even though she knew instinctively that it was Kyle. He stood beside her, a grin on his face, and two glasses of wine in his hands, one held out to her.

She took it and drank back a sip.

"I was just thinking that so much has changed while I've been away." She glanced at him. "And so much hasn't."

His gaze was heavy on hers for a moment, until he tipped his head, motioning toward the orchard. "Care for a walk?"

She considered the alternative. Was square dancing with her sister or watching her cousins sway happily with their boyfriends her idea of a good time? As much as she'd missed them, it wasn't. And being with Kyle...Well, it was as easy and comfortable as it had always been.

"I haven't been here since I got back to town," she said by way of an excuse for falling into step beside him. "I always loved this place."

"It's the heart of this town," he agreed. "Certainly the center of your family. And it was also where you and I started our life together."

She swallowed hard. It wasn't where they'd gotten married, but it held just as much significance. It was where he'd proposed.

"You certainly surprised me," she said, thinking back on that brisk fall day when she'd been helping with the harvest, tired and hungry, and looking forward to a nice dinner in town. Kyle had been there, along with her sisters and cousins, and they were still in that full bloom of love, where her heart sped up every time their eyes met, where the anticipation of being alone with him hadn't lost its thrill.

"Let's take a walk," she said now, out loud. She glanced at him. "That's what you said."

Just like tonight, she realized, with a start.

"You couldn't resist my charms back then." Kyle nudged her playfully, and against her better judgment, she felt herself relaxing into the moment, into the memory that only they had shared.

"You didn't even have a ring." Not that it mattered. Instead, he'd twisted one from the grapevines, told her it was temporary, that he couldn't wait another moment to start their lives together, to dream about their future.

"The real ring came later," he pointed out, and she nodded.

"But that first ring was still the most special." With a frown, she wondered what had happened to it. She'd been so careful to set it aside, once the small solitaire diamond was safely on her finger.

"If I could go back and do it all over again, that's the one part I wouldn't change." Kyle stopped walking and turned to look at her.

Brooke's heart was beating so loudly now that she was sure he could hear it, out here in the fields, where it was just the two of them.

"Me either," she said, knowing that it was true. That despite how it had all turned out, if she had the choice to do it all over again, she would, because that was a time in her life when she was genuinely, truly happy.

And she couldn't be sure she'd ever felt that way again. Or ever would.

Kyle reached down and took her hand, and she stiffened at his touch, wanting to pull it back almost as much as she wanted to give in to this moment.

"I took your hand, and I said something to the effect of...Will you marry me?" He laughed, and she joined him, even though tears were forming in her eyes, just as they had that day. Only now they weren't happy tears. They were bittersweet.

"I was so nervous that I honestly don't even remember."

"I remember," Brooke said softly. "You said, I don't have anything to offer you right now but my open hand, and a promise..." She swallowed hard, unable to finish the words that he'd spoken to her that night.

"And a promise," he said now, his eyes staring deep into hers. "And a promise to always love you."

The last words must have been spoken a hundred times throughout their relationship, maybe a thousand, but it had been so long now since she'd heard them, believed them, felt them. She could remember his words. But she couldn't remember how it felt to be loved by him. Until now.

She slowly pulled her hand free, pressing it against the skirt of her sundress, hating how cold and empty it now felt.

"I should get back. My sisters will be wondering where I am. I promised I'd dance with Gabby." She laughed to cover her nervous energy.

"Or you can dance with me instead?"

He couldn't be serious. The entire room would no doubt freeze in place to see Kyle Harrison and Brooke Conway sharing the dance floor.

But that wasn't the real reason she didn't want to dance with him. She didn't trust herself in his arms. Not after tonight.

"I have to get going soon," she said, quickening her pace back to the barn.

"That's fine," he said as they reached the open doors, where the glow of lights made her see the amusement shining in his eyes. "You can save it for a rain check."

She narrowed her eyes on him. "Rain check?"

"The prom committee needs chaperones for next weekend. I signed us up." He took a sip of the wine he was still holding as if this was the most natural thing he could have said.

She blinked at him. "You can't be serious."

"Very serious. Looks like I've got a date to the prom. Again." He just grinned and walked back inside the barn, leaving her to stand outside and stare up at the night sky, and wonder if she would ever be free of this man.

Or if she really wanted to be.

13

On the following Saturday afternoon, Brooke stared into the contents of her closet and for the tenth time talked herself out of asking Gabby to stop by. Ironic, she knew, to be seeking fashion advice when she was the one who designed dresses for a living. But what did you wear to a school prom with your ex-husband? What did you wear to a school prom at her age? Gabby had been right when she'd pointed out that Brooke often overdressed for life in Blue Harbor.

That she'd forgotten the ways. That maybe, she no longer fit in.

Eventually, Brooke decided on a black shift dress, knowing that she could never regret a classic. She paired it with strappy gold sandals with a kitten heel, and a chunky gold necklace, lest she look too prim. Her hair she swept back with a clip, and for makeup, she kept it minimal. They were technically chaperones, after all. This wasn't a date, no matter what Kyle insisted on calling it.

Still, she felt a flutter of anticipation at the thought of spending another evening with him. She'd kept busy all week, managed not to give tonight too much thought, but now there was no denying the fact that she was going back to the very high school where she and Kyle had first fallen in love, where he'd be waiting for her.

She set a hand to her stomach as it tightened at that thought, and grabbed a beaded gold clutch before heading out the door.

The school was close enough to walk to, even in the shoes, and despite the threat of blisters, she hurried her pace, not that she was in any rush. She swept her eyes up and down Main Street, knowing that her sisters and cousins and probably everyone else in town would find out about how she was spending her evening before this time tomorrow, but by then it would be over and done with. And right now, she didn't want to explain why she was dressed for a night out, and not a night at the Carriage House Inn Pub or dinner at the café, or even the Yacht Club. No, she was dressed for a special event.

And this was starting to feel like a special event, not just because it was the school prom.

Her sister Gabby would appreciate it, though. She'd been on the prom planning committee, even if she'd never gone to the dance, other than to set it up. Brooke had, of course, though. Had the pictures to prove it, somewhere. Beside her, giggling girls who looked so much younger than she had ever been scurried excitedly along the sidewalk, wobbling in their heels, leaving a waft of perfume in their wake. The outside of the school was decorated with balloons and signs and…flowers.

Brooke gulped and stopped walking, realizing with a beating heart that of course there would be flowers. This was the school prom! And who else would be in charge of the centerpieces other than...

"Gabby!" She called out to her sister as she appeared in the open doorway, wearing jeans and a tee-shirt and balancing a large floral arrangement by its glass vase.

Gabby followed the sound and her gaze landed on Brooke in confusion. "Brooke?" She raked a look over Brooke's attire. "What are you doing here?"

"I was asked to help chaperone," Brooke said as she neared. She felt suddenly self-conscious of her attire until she realized that Gabby was part of the setup committee, and would be leaving before the event kicked off. "I should have known that you'd be part of this."

"You know how much I love to plan a good prom." Gabby laughed and then gave a little sigh. It was still a sore spot that no one had ever asked her to the biggest high school event of the spring. "Britt roped you in, huh?"

Gabby didn't wait for an answer, and Brooke took the time to peek inside the open doors to see her cousin giving instructions to a group of students, who were already dressed for the event and probably eager to get on with the fun.

"Well, I'd ask you to give me a hand with these arrangements, but I'd hate for you to get your dress dirty." Gabby brushed a wisp of hair from her face and then pointed at Brooke's dress. "By the way, I'm borrowing that if I'm ever asked out on a date."

Brooke grinned. "Deal. And I'm happy to help. This is a very forgiving fabric."

"If you're sure," Gabby said, but she wasted no time in marching to her delivery van and handing Brooke one of the remaining arrangements.

Brooke tucked her beaded clutch under her arm so she could manage the vase without spilling any of the water. It was a cheerful arrangement, made of bright purple flowers with a touch of pink mixed in.

"It's weird being back here, isn't it?" Gabby asked as they walked into the school and down the corridor that had once been so familiar and still bore the same scent of cleaning detergent and…well, probably sweat.

"It's certainly a blast from the past," Brooke commented, as they passed by the fine arts studio where she'd spent many happy afternoons, and came to a stop outside the gymnasium doors.

"Speaking of a blast from the past." Gabby nudged her chin. "Look who's here."

Brooke's pulse skipped as she looked across the gymnasium, which had been converted to a spring forest, with trees, and fairy lights, and bunches of big, bright bouquets on the center of each round table. Even though she knew that Kyle would be here, she still felt a rush of warmth spread through her when she saw him standing near the concessions stand, his hands in the pockets of his grey slacks, his suit coat buttoned. He turned, slowly, as if feeling her stare, his face breaking out into a grin when he caught her eye.

"My, my," Gabby said, sliding her a pointed look. "Looks like you might have a date to this prom after all."

Brooke felt her cheeks flush and knew that there was no sense in hiding it from Gabby. "You know that Kyle and I can't get back together."

Gabby scoffed at that. "Why not? People break up and get back together all the time." She set an arrangement on a nearby table and fluffed a few of the flowers. "I mean, I wouldn't know from personal experience, but look at Britt and Robbie, and Amelia and Matt."

"It's different. Kyle and I are—were—married." Her heart sped up and she wondered briefly if Gabby had caught on, but her sister was too focused on her flowers to catch the slip or read anything into it.

"In my opinion that just means your bond is even deeper." Gabby took the arrangement from Brooke's hand and sauntered away with a knowing smile, leaving Brooke with no choice but to square her shoulders and cross the room.

Kyle grinned as she approached. "Am I allowed to tell you that you look beautiful tonight?"

Brooke looked down at her feet, her pink-painted toenails peeping out of her shoes, and then back up into his eyes. "You clean up pretty well yourself," she said.

And he did. The last time she'd seen him this dressed up must have been their wedding day, she realized with a start. He'd worn a navy suit, crisp white shirt, and a navy bowtie. It wasn't like his typical style of jeans and a tee-shirt or sweater, and as she'd walked down the aisle on her father's arm, she remembered thinking that he'd dressed up for her because this wasn't just her day, it was their day. Just like her future was supposed to be their future. For so long, everything she did, every plan she made, every dream she had, included him.

It was too easy to get used to that feeling again, to fall into old habits, to pretend that the part of their past that had driven them apart never happened.

"Punch?" Kyle asked, breaking the silence.

Brooke nodded eagerly, even though she wasn't even thirsty, and her hands were feeling a little shaky, too. "Sure."

He ladled some of the pink drink into a plastic cup and handed it to her as the band began to play and the kids began to filter in, the girls in long gowns that were all of a sleeker style than the frilly and poufy options Brooke and her friends had gone with all those years ago, the boys looking suitably uncomfortable in their formalwear, tugging at their ties, or skimming the screens of their phones, trying to look otherwise occupied.

Brooke couldn't help but laugh. "They're children!"

Kyle grinned as he looked on. "Yep, and we were too once." He hesitated before giving her a rueful glance. "Remember our senior prom?"

"Ha!" Brooke took a sip of her drink. "You gave me a corsage that was nearly the size of the table centerpieces."

"The bigger the better." He shook his head. "I didn't know what I was doing back then." After a beat, he sobered, his eyes softened when they met hers. "Maybe I never did."

Her heart thawed another notch. "It was sweet. And it certainly got a lot of attention. I had the prettiest flowers of every girl at the dance. Though it did make things a little awkward when it came to actually dancing."

He laughed. "I do remember that."

She remembered something else, too. How she'd saved it. Tucked it away to dry out and cherish. A keepsake of a magical night.

A night that now felt so long ago, even if the rush of emotions was coming at her as if it were yesterday.

They fell into silence as the crowd filled the room and the kids lined up for punch and cookies, groups of girls who hadn't attended with dates sat at tables chatting, and already some of the couples were on the dance floor, swaying to the music.

"You're not wearing a corsage tonight," Kyle eventually said, motioning to her wrist.

She stared at him, unsure of his implication until she saw the glimmer in his eyes as he jutted his chin toward the dance floor.

"Oh." She stiffened. "No. I mean, aren't we supposed to be watching the kids?"

Kyle gave a dismissive shrug. "Look at them. What's the worst thing that can happen? Someone spikes the punch?"

Brooke blinked. "Well, yes, that."

He laughed. "Come on, Brooke, have a little fun. For old time's sake."

She hesitated, knowing that she would have a hard time fighting him off when he was looking at her like that, his grin mischievous and inviting, his fingers waggling her toward him. He wasn't going to take no for an answer, but then, when had he ever? When Kyle wanted something, he made it happen.

Which was why it hurt so damn much to think that he hadn't wanted to stay with her, to come with her to New York, to go through with the plans they had made. Together.

"Just one dance. You did promise me that."

His arm skimmed hers to take her hand. It felt warm, solid, and achingly familiar. It felt like coming home.

"We promised each other a lot of things," she said, feeling tense and defensive.

Silence stretched between them as the band tuned their instruments for the next song, and she could feel the rise and fall of her chest as her heart beat in her chest. There were too many memories in this room, too many good parts of the past that kept pulling her back, to another time and another place.

And maybe this was what he wanted. To think of all the good between them, and not the bad. To hold onto it, rather than let it go.

Or maybe just to enjoy it, one last time.

The band picked up again, and Kyle gave her a lopsided grin. "They're playing our song."

"I thought our song was by that British band—" she started to say, but he squeezed her hand tighter.

"Come on, Brooke. What's one more dance?"

One more, or one last? Suddenly, she didn't want to know.

"One," she said firmly. "And only because it beats standing next to the punch bowl, feeling like an old lady."

"You're the same age as me!" He laughed.

"You don't think that's old to these kids?" she chided.

She waited for him to drop her hand now that she was following him onto the dance floor, but he showed no signs of it, and instead gave her one graceful twirl before wrapping his free hand around her waist and pulling her close.

She blanched. It was their wedding dance. The very entry that they had rehearsed over and over after three lessons at the dance studio, the one that had been greeted with a roar of applause by their friends and family. But the song...the song was familiar, now, as she listened to the words. It was the first song that they had ever danced to, long before prom, when they were still two gangly teens, before everything got complicated.

She closed her eyes and listened to the music, trying not to focus on the beat of Kyle's heart against her own, on the way his body felt pressed against hers, at the way he sang softly in her ear, just like he had on their wedding night, and every night that they had rehearsed their moves, laughing at first, before falling into a steady rhythm.

She'd been so happy. Life had felt so full. Her entire future felt so certain.

And then...

She pulled away, shaking her head. Kyle stared at her, looking bewildered.

"Is something wrong?"

"Of course something is wrong!" she heard herself snap. "Everything is wrong, Kyle. This is wrong. You and me, dancing like nothing ever happened. Like the past six years never happened. Like I didn't move away."

"Like I didn't stay back," he finished. His jaw tensed. "Brooke, I didn't do this to upset you."

She blinked away the tears that threatened to spill, not wanting to make a scene, even if a quick glance around reassured her that none of these kids were looking at the thirty-somethings in the room. They had their own romantic woes to worry about.

She caught herself on that thought. There was no romance left between her and Kyle. That had ended a very long time ago, and it never should have been revisited.

"I need some air," she said, breaking away from him. She grabbed her clutch, pushing around tables and girls in chiffon dresses, desperate to get out the doors of the gym, this school, maybe even this town.

Her heels were loud in the empty corridor, but the door creaked open loudly behind her, just as she knew it would.

"Why won't you let this go?" she asked, whipping around to face him. "You and I were over a long time ago."

He pushed his hands into his pockets, giving her a long, uncertain look. "Because it wasn't easy to let you go, Brooke. And...I guess it still isn't."

He had her there. Managed to snag her breath away. She stared at him, feeling unbalanced and unsure.

"But...you never came after me. You didn't try to stop me."

"Is that what you really wanted? For me to tell you not to go?" His expression looked pained. "Going to New York had been your dream. Our dream," he corrected himself softly. "Just because I had to give it up, didn't mean you should."

Her mouth felt dry, and her head was spinning. All this time she'd assumed he'd never supported her, when it turned out, maybe that was never true at all.

But one thing was, she thought, hardening her resolve. "You didn't have to give it up, Kyle. You chose to give up our dream, our plan." She swallowed hard. "Us. You chose to give up on us."

"You think that was easy?" He'd raised his voice, anger pushing through the sadness that hung between them, like a weight that they couldn't shed. "I didn't feel I had a choice at the time. I didn't see another way. I had an obligation."

"And I wasn't an obligation? I was your wife."

"And he was my father!" Kyle ground out.

Brooke closed her mouth. She couldn't argue with that. And much as it still hurt her now, a part of her also understood it.

"I waited for you, you know," she said, surprised at herself for admitting this. Once, she had been so mad at Kyle that she couldn't bear the thought of him knowing just how many nights she'd cried for him, longed for him. Missed him.

And wondered if she hadn't made the biggest mistake of her life.

"You never called," he said.

She raised her eyebrows. "You didn't either."

"I didn't think you wanted me to," Kyle said, giving a little grin that showed no amusement.

Her heart felt heavy, thinking of all the time they'd lost. Of all that might have been. Could have been.

And maybe, should have been.

"Why did you never come back to town?" he asked suddenly, looking her square in the eye. "Oh, I heard you stopped through once for a few days. But other than that you stayed away."

"Because of you!" she cried, exasperated. "Because of this. You and me. And what we had. And because it hurt, Kyle. And it still hurts."

His gaze was tender and understanding, and she saw her own pain reflected in his eyes as he stepped toward her and slowly took her hand. His skin was warm, smooth, and achingly familiar.

"Kyle," she whispered, but he looked at her, lacing his fingers through hers, saying nothing, because really, there was nothing to say. They'd said everything. They understood. They didn't only share a history. They'd shared a loss, too.

He leaned down and kissed her, just like he had a thousand times before, and this time it was no different. It was one effortless, lingering, soft kiss. She'd taken so many of them for granted, assumed that there would always be another. Until there wasn't. One day, without maybe even realizing it, they'd had their very last kiss.

Until tonight.

She backed away slowly, biting down on her lip, wanting to savor the sensation as much as she knew she should try to forget it. Because oh, she had tried so hard to forget him, these moments. These feelings.

And maybe that was exactly what she should do. Go back to New York. Forget this night ever happened.

And somehow, find a way to forget Kyle again too.

14

Brooke woke Sunday morning to the sound of the birds chirping on the tree outside her open window. Despite the restless sleep she'd had, she couldn't help but smile. Back in New York, she would have woken to the honking horns of frustrated cab drivers and the wail of sirens. She'd forgotten about the simple pleasures of nature that her hometown offered. She'd forgotten about a lot of things.

Or tried to forget, at least.

She lay in bed for a while as the sunlight filled her room, knowing that she most definitely needed curtains and soon, but not today. No, today she had too much on her mind—all the work she planned to do in her shop to prepare for tomorrow, and of course…

She closed her eyes and replayed the kiss, feeling her heart race as she relived the memory. It had happened, and she wasn't so sure that she regretted it. And that was…confusing.

Eventually, because she was going to drive herself crazy thinking about last night any longer, she pushed back the duvet and showered and dressed for the day. A little fresh air would do her some good, but instead of walking, she decided to try her old bicycle, for old times' sake. She laughed as she climbed on and began a shaky push down the road, thankful that traffic was light. How long had it been since she'd felt the wind in her face, the rush of gaining speed when she hit a small decline?

She took the path by the lakefront, enjoying the view, and making a promise to herself to get out to Evening Island soon, in time to see the lilacs bloom.

She didn't make the conscious decision to pedal north and turn onto the gravel road where she'd once lived. The pull of curiosity was nearly as steep as her reservation, but it won out, and before she could change her mind, she'd turned onto the tree-lined street that had drawn her in at first sight, with its small homes tucked behind large oaks and maples.

And there, where the road ended, was her house. Or rather, Kyle's house.

It was smaller than she'd remembered but neat and tidy with fresh white paint and a dark blue door. She slowed her pace, slanting a glance as she went past, planning to just turn around, and darn it if a squirrel didn't choose that moment to dash out into the road, startling her and making her jerk her handlebars. Her front tire caught a large rock, forcing the bike to an abrupt stop. Only quick thinking prevented her from toppling to the side, but the brush with the grass twisted her ankle, causing her to yelp in pain.

The front door of the house swung open, and there was Kyle, taking in the scene as he sipped from a mug of coffee.

He looked surprised to see her, but not displeased, and all at once, Brooke knew that this was a bad idea. Something had shifted between them, and it had been so much easier when their relationship was defined, even if it was still murky in the legal sense.

Brooke tried to put some weight on her ankle and winced in pain. There would be no pedaling back to town at this rate, much less walking the bike. Against her better judgment, she said, "Do you have an ice pack?"

"Come on in," he said with a little grin. "It's still your house."

She wasn't so sure about that, and she certainly didn't think of it that way, either. She'd left this house within two months of married life, making a home of her shabby city apartment instead, but as she reluctantly toed the kickstand on her bike and began a slow walk to the front porch, she felt as if no time had passed at all since she'd lived here.

She could still remember the day they'd found it, just a few short months before their wedding. It had come on the market as a rental, which seemed like the perfect solution for their long-term plans. Sure, it had needed work, which was why it wasn't attracting tourists and was well within their price range, but the owner said they could do with it as they pleased, and besides, it was only supposed to be temporary.

But even though it was short-lived, it was special. A little piece of the world that was theirs and theirs alone. The first kitchen she'd cooked in, the first dining room where they'd shared meals, as proper adults at their own table—a concept that felt so strange and exciting at the time.

Still, it wasn't her home any more than her apartment above the shop was his. She walked up the familiar path, or hobbled, really, and clenched her teeth against the pain as she took the steps. She knew if she showed any weakness, Kyle would step in, put an arm around her, and she wasn't sure she could resist his touch another time.

Wasn't sure she wanted to, she thought, catching his eye as she reached the door.

"I haven't ridden a bike in years," she said ruefully.

"Some things take a little getting used to, but once you get the hang of it, it's like you never stopped." His eyes locked hers, and she swallowed hard against the pounding of her chest. She had the feeling that he wasn't talking about the bicycle right now.

"I can't believe you still live in this place. It feels like yesterday that we were moving in." Their friends and family had all pitched in, even though their belongings were meager. A hand-me-down sofa, a coffee table that Kyle had made himself, a mattress until he was finished carving the headboard.

"Remember how I carried you over the threshold?" Kyle said now as she took the final step onto the porch.

She resisted a smile, but not for long. "You tripped on that loose board and nearly killed us both." She laughed at the memory. She hadn't thought of it in a long time.

"Well, it's all fixed now," Kyle said quietly.

Brooke was preparing herself for the fading carpet, the walls that could have used a fresh coat of paint, the nail holes that she strategically covered in cheap framed art prints.

Instead, she was met with stained hardwood floors, crisp walls in a warm neutral color, and sunlight billowing in through the windows, where her curtains still hung.

"It looks amazing," she gasped, taking it all in. "We talked about doing all this, remember? If we held onto the place, for when we visited."

"For when we came back," he said, nodding. "I remember. I remember everything."

She pulled her eyes from his, tearing herself from the memories that were washing over her in waves.

"You didn't take down the curtains," she whispered. They were prettier than she remembered, and now she knew why she'd had to ask for the fabric for a gift. It hadn't been cheap, and back then, had certainly been outside of her budget.

With the changes that Kyle had made to the space, they fit better than ever before.

"You worked too hard on those to ever take them down," he said, giving her a hint of a smile. He jutted his chin to the floor. "Believe it or not, this wood was under the carpet the whole time. And the paint, well, it's just a fresh coat."

"It's…wonderful," she said, venturing farther inside to realize that other than unleashing everything that was already there, the house was the same as it had been the day she'd left.

"Better than the apartment you found in New York?" He raised an eyebrow, clearly remembering the conversation they'd had about the place. Of course, it had looked much different in the pictures than it had in real life.

"I cried the first night there," she admitted now with a little smile, and not because of him. "It took a lot of time to fix up and make my own."

Her own. He nodded at this, and the room fell silent. She used the opportunity to look around, at the mantle, which he'd replaced with one of his carvings, at the framed photo that rested on it.

Their wedding photo.

He followed her gaze. "Didn't seem right to shove it in a box or a drawer."

She didn't know what to say to that, but one thing was very obvious. "I thought you didn't do woodworking anymore."

She looked at him, questioningly, and he walked into the adjacent kitchen, pulled some ice from the freezer, and dropped it into a plastic bag. "This stuff, it was just for me."

She looked at the dining table, the one that been his gift to her, seeing it with fresh eyes. There was so much care, and detail, from the turned legs to the grain of the wood.

"You have a real talent, Kyle," she said, letting her gaze drift back to him. "I wish you wouldn't give it all up."

His mouth was firm, his eyes sad. "Running the pub takes a lot of time. The business is struggling, but I don't need to tell you that."

No, he didn't.

"I never wanted the pub to fail," she said softly.

"And I never wanted to run it," he replied, shocking her. It was the first admittance. In the past, he had always been so defensive, so determined to prove to himself that he was making the right choice, even when she knew that he wouldn't be happy.

Now, realizing that he wasn't, she didn't feel any better.

She looked out the window, out onto the trees that led to the glimpse of the lake, to the rocky shoreline where the two chairs that he'd made still sat.

"I used to love sitting out there, watching the waves, dreaming about our life together."

He came to stand beside her at the counter, following her gaze. "We had a lot of plans. But there was another plan, too. Do you remember it?"

A chill rolled over her as she stared out the window, thinking of him beside her, so content, the breeze on their faces, a mug of coffee in his hand, just like right now, like any other morning.

"We always said that after we'd made it, gone out into the world and done all we'd planned to do, that we'd find a way back to this house, and we'd live out our golden years sitting right there on those chairs."

Tears prickled the back of her eyes, blurring her vision, and she looked away, quickly wiping at her cheeks with her back turned to him.

"Oh, I'm not sure we ever really meant it," she said casually, even though she knew it wasn't true. That it had been another grand plan, another pipe dream, more like it. "That would have required buying this place."

"I did buy it," he said flatly, forcing her attention.

She stared at him for a moment, not sure of what to say. "Oh. Wow."

Technically, she supposed that did make it their home.

"I should have told you," he admitted now, sighing heavily. "It's all in my name, but I still should have said something. The owner gave a good deal, sort of a rent to own arrangement."

She shook her head, knowing that it was important, that she should know, but at the same time, she wasn't sure that it mattered. If she counted their night at the barn dance, then there was only one date left on their agreement until they went their separate ways forever, in every sense of the word.

"I'm glad you kept it," she said, thinking that it would have stung to know some other couple had snatched it up, made a home of it, lived a life that she had given up or never found.

He heaved a sigh. "Not so sure I'll be keeping it for long."

She frowned at him. "What do you mean?"

"The pub is underwater. I'm sure that doesn't surprise you."

Her shoulders dropped when she saw the disappointment in his eyes. "So you'll need to cash out the house to save the business?"

"Something like that," he said, turning his back to pull together some ice in a bag.

Brooke walked around the small space, toward the dining table, running her hands softly over the grooves of the wood, the stain was even more rich and beautiful than she'd remembered. She smiled, about to tell him so, when something caught her eye.

A stack of papers, with the bank's letterhead.

Loan papers, she realized with a start.

She inched closer as her heart began to race, scanning quickly, until she looked up, seeing Kyle staring at her, his expression pained.

"You're applying for a loan for the pub?" It was all there, in black and white, but somehow still she needed to hear him say it because he knew what this meant every bit as much as she did. A business loan wasn't easy to get, worse when you had two people in the same family trying for one, and he'd known it all along.

"Ryan thinks the only way to keep the pub going is to change it."

"And you?"

He shrugged. "Guess my problem has always been the same. I can't let go of the past, even when I know I should."

He held her gaze for so long that her heart felt like it had dropped into her stomach. Standing here, in this house—in their home—she felt like she had gone back to the past. Never left it.

And maybe that's what she should have done.

"Good thing we're getting divorced then," she quipped, but damn it, there was an edge to her tone and the tears threatened the back of her eyes.

"Brooke. This wasn't my idea. This wasn't part of the plan when you first came back."

"And since when do you stick to plans, Kyle?" The tears in her eyes were hot now, threatening to fall, and she didn't even try to stop them as she pushed past him and down the porch steps, ignoring the pain in her ankle. It would mend—but her heart...it never had. It was just like that awful day, the last time she was here, when he'd told her he wasn't coming to New York, that he'd made his decision, that he was staying right here.

That something else was more important to him than a future with her.

She'd packed her bags, knowing there wasn't much she wanted to take, that she was looking to her future now, that anything from the past would only hold her back. She'd sat in the bedroom, on the old faded quilt, letting the tears silently fall, willing him to come inside and tell her to stay as much as she willed him to come in and tell her he had changed his mind.

Instead, she'd heard the opening and the closing of the back door, and she'd quietly slipped the thin bands off her finger, and set them down on the bedside table, before walking out the front door, and not looking back.

Kyle stepped toward her now, but she moved back quickly.

It was a mistake kissing him. Just like it was a mistake coming here.

Maybe, it was a mistake coming back to this town.

*

Dinner with her family was the last thing Brooke was up to tonight, but she'd spent too many years alone in an apartment to do the same again. She arrived early and told her mother that she'd be looking through the attic for any old pieces of furniture that might be used in her apartment. The truth was that she needed to be alone, to think, but she also needed to do something she'd avoided for years.

Face the past.

Her mother had kept a trunk for each of the girls, where she kept their baby blankets and school yearbooks, treasures that they might someday want to keep, junk that she as a mother couldn't readily part with, no matter how inconsequential it now seemed.

Brooke dropped onto the wooden floor and opened the chest, her heart thudding at what she already knew would be inside, but it sank just the same when she pushed the top back, revealed her tulle veil, carefully resting on her satin wedding gown.

She stared at the dress for a minute, realizing that it was more beautiful than she'd remembered it, or perhaps given it credit. Or maybe she hadn't wanted to remember how perfect it had been.

Or how perfect Kyle was, either.

For a little while, at least.

She closed the trunk and set it to the side, vowing to take it into her shop when she left tonight. She lived in Blue Harbor now, and she owned a bridal shop. This belonged with her more now than it did inside a dusty attic, even if it hurt too much to look at it.

The trunk felt heavy as she moved it to the side, heavier than its contents should weigh, at first glance. Curious, she opened the lid again and carefully slid her hand under the skirt of the dress, her fingers finding something leather. Her wedding album.

She knew she could close the lid again. Shove the entire trunk back in its place. Pretend she'd never sought it out, never found anything related to her past.

Instead, she carefully set the dress on an old armchair and pulled the album free. She ran her fingertips over the ivory cover. The date of their union was embossed with gold, and as she turned it open to reveal the first page, she felt a lump form in her throat at what she saw. Two smiling people, holding hands, looking into each other's eyes. It was a black and white shot, but even still, she could see the radiance in her face, the joy in Kyle's smile. The promise of so much ahead of them.

Until it had all taken a turn.

She swallowed back the tears that prickled her eyes, not wanting them to fall and ruin the still-capture. The proof that once upon a time all that she had needed to make her happy was Kyle.

That he had been enough.

And that she couldn't remember the last time she had smiled like that again, since leaving for New York. Or coming back.

There was more in the trunk, too. Yearbooks with yellowing pages, a plastic box containing her senior prom corsage, now so dried out and brittle she was nearly afraid to handle it. Loose photos were scattered in a shoebox and she leafed through them, smiling at the memories of long summer afternoons on the water with her sisters, and crisp fall days at the orchard with her cousins.

But there was more. A napkin from the ice cream parlor with a date scrawled at the bottom. She held it closer in the dim light, trying to discern the handwriting, not recognizing it as her own, until she realized that it wasn't her handwriting, but it was equally familiar all the same. It was Kyle's. And there, in black ink, was the proof of their first date.

At Harborside Creamery.

She remembered now. She'd ordered the raspberry ice cream, and he'd bought her the largest size, even back then, making her self-conscious, but happy all the same because it meant it would take longer to eat, and that meant more time in his company. And she'd wondered if he'd thought of that too. If it had been part of his plan.

If it had been part of his plan last time they'd gone, too.

Quickly, she looked through the rest of the souvenirs: movie ticket stubs and strips of photos from the booth at the bowling alley of her and Kyle in silly poses, looking so happy that it made her laugh out loud.

And there, under a trinket he'd won for her at the Summer in the Square festival one year, was another napkin. This one from the café, before it was owned by Amelia, back when going to a restaurant on their own felt like a big deal. And there, in the corner, was another marking. Another date, only it was blurred out, and the paper was stiff, as if it had been caught in the rain.

She closed her eyes, remembering now. Their first kiss had been in the rain, right after their first dinner at the café. It had come down while they were walking down Main Street, and they hadn't thought to bring an umbrella. They'd run for Kyle's car, shielding themselves with what little they had on them until they'd given up, standing at the corner under the streetlamp, their hair drenched, the rain falling into their eyes. And he'd told her she'd never looked prettier. And she believed him. Because that was the thing about Kyle. He always made her think of her best self. He'd always made her reach for her dreams.

She set the two napkins to the side, knowing what she would find next, because it was all there now, every small piece of their history. She remembered. And as she picked up the napkin for Fiorre's, she knew that he did too.

That he hadn't just asked her out on six dates.

He'd planned them.

"You up here?" There was a knock at the open door, followed by heavy footsteps. It was Gabby, already climbing the wooden stairs to the attic.

Brooke quickly set everything back in the chest and wiped her eyes, but there was no time to hide the evidence.

"Memory lane," Gabby observed, coming to stand next to her. She sneezed, and then sneezed again.

"I was up here looking for old furniture I might use in my apartment," Brooke explained.

Gabby didn't look convinced. "And you happened to find your bridal trunk, complete with your wedding album and every other high school memento that Mom can't bring herself to toss?"

Brooke looked down at it. "I'm sort of glad she didn't."

Gabby reached out a hand and took the album, smiling as she turned the pages. "I forgot how beautiful that dress was."

"I did too," Brooke admitted, letting her gaze rest on it. "I was so busy dreaming of bigger and more exciting things, I don't think I realized how wonderful I had it."

"Are we talking about the dress or something else?" Gabby asked, giving her a look of suspicion.

Brooke ran her fingers over the skirt of the gown and let her arm drop. "It wasn't easy for me to leave, you know."

Gabby's expression stiffened. "We never thought it was."

"And New York...it had a lot to offer. But not you, or Jenna, or Mom and Dad.

"Or Kyle."

Brooke looked back at the trunk and all the memories it held. "Kyle and I weren't meant to be. Other things in life always got in the way."

"But that's all in the past," Gabby insisted. Ever the romantic. "The future is wide open."

Was it? Once, Brooke had felt that way, when she and Kyle were dreaming of their life together. But those dreams were separate, and ultimately, it was those dreams that drove them apart.

"It doesn't have to be all or nothing anymore, does it?" Gabby scooted forward. "I get it. I do. You wanted to go to the city, Kyle wanted to stay here. But now you don't have to make that choice."

Brooke thought of the loan and her plans for the shop. Of Kyle's plans for the pub.

"I'm not sure it's that simple," she said sadly, because oh, how she wished it was.

"If love was simple, I'd be married by now," Gabby joked, lightening the mood. "It wasn't all bad, Brooke."

Brooke gave a little smile. "No. It wasn't. I guess my memory was tainted by...everything." She took the album back and carefully set it in the trunk.

"It was a beautiful wedding. The flowers weren't too shabby either," Gabby remarked with a grin. They were part of her early efforts, with shades of apricot and cream that had been the perfect complement to the navy bridesmaid dresses.

"They were perfect," Brooke said quietly.

"But you know what really sticks out to me?" Gabby continued, even though Brooke was standing up now, wanting to end this conversation, wishing that she'd never come up here at all and had instead made do with the furniture she had or ordered something online.

"What's that?" she said flatly, shifting aside Jenna's old clarinet case. Piano had definitely been her calling.

"How happy you looked," Gabby said.

Brooke didn't want to mention that she noticed it too.

"You know, you're pretty lucky, Brooke," Gabby said.

Brooke frowned at her. "Let me remind you that my marriage ended, rather quickly, too."

"But you were happy, even if it was short-lived," Gabby said. "You were in love, truly, deeply in love, and you were loved back. And that's not something everyone can say."

Brooke knew that Gabby was referring to herself. She also knew that her sister had a point.

"Candy was in my shop this week," Gabby said.

Brooke hoped they were shifting the conversation back to Candy's endless indecision, but Gabby gave her a knowing look and said, "She told me about you and Kyle having dinner at the café."

Brooke brushed a hand through the air, even though her cheeks were hot. "It was just two old friends catching up."

"Is that all you want to be? Friends?"

Brooke thought about that for a moment. Until recently, she wouldn't have even thought they could be that much to each other anymore, but her anger had faded, landing somewhere been acceptance and resignation.

"Maybe it's all we can be." She'd moved on. And now, she realized, thinking of the plans that Kyle had made, he had too.

15

Kyle had managed to avoid Ryan for days thanks to an uptick in customers mostly due to the tourists filling the more desirable spots in the town. By midweek, though, he knew there was no sense in pushing things off any longer.

He finished washing down the bar and turning over the chairs, then went back to the small office that his father used to sit in, right off the kitchen, which had been dark for hours since they stopped serving food by nine.

"Ready to talk?" he asked, coming to drop onto the spare chair in the corner, next to the filing cabinet that bore years of receipts and tax information, in case they were ever audited. He'd always told himself he'd go through it sometime, clear out the unnecessary paperwork, and get rid of the clutter. Instead, he'd managed to toss a dried-out houseplant. For the most part, he'd stayed clear of this room. There was too much history here, even for him.

Ryan looked up in surprise and closed his laptop, showing that he was giving Kyle his full attention.

Kyle pushed out a breath. It was time to get this off his chest. This time, with no regrets.

"I'm not selling the house." There. It was out.

Ryan nodded thoughtfully, not revealing any emotion. Still, Kyle felt the need to explain.

"I've put my entire adult life into this pub. I've given up a lot for it. And I tried my best to keep it running, the only way I knew how. The way I thought that Dad would have wanted it done." He chewed the inside of his mouth. This wasn't easy, but then, nothing about any of this had ever been easy. "It's still hard not to feel like I've let Dad down in a way. He loved this place."

He looked around, at the stacks of paperwork, the odd coffee mug resting on the file cabinet. Another on the desk.

Ryan gave him a small smile. "You did more for this pub than I ever did. More for Dad too. I never said it before, but I owe you an apology, Kyle. It was because of you that I was able to keep my job, keep my relationship for a while at least, and still know that when I came home everything would be exactly as it was when I left."

"Right down to the limited customers and the stale menu and the dark ambiance?" Kyle said wryly.

"I never said it when Dad died, but it would have killed me to lose this place, too. It was never my thing because it was always Dad's thing...with you."

Now it was Kyle's turn to look surprised. "I don't follow."

"Dad was always a dreamer. Yeah, he probably didn't have the best business sense, and this place was in trouble long before you took over. It made me crazy, really. Made me want to go into business, work with numbers, and facts. But you...you're a lot like Dad. Dad followed his heart, and you did too."

Kyle swallowed hard. His heart was with Brooke. And he hadn't followed her anywhere.

"I don't want to lose this place," he said gruffly. "I never did."

"Then let me have a stab at it. I'd like to have a chance to make Dad proud too. In...my own way."

Kyle pulled back. "You mean that?"

"I owe him that," Ryan said. "And...I owe it to you, too."

"I don't know what to say," Kyle said. He felt suddenly lost, as directionless as he ever had in his life. For as long as he could remember, there had been a plan, first with Brooke, and then, when his Dad died, to keep this place going. It was all right there in front of him.

Now he was free. To do as he wanted. To carve his own path. And he wasn't even sure where to begin. Or if it was too late.

"You don't need to say anything," Ryan said. "Honestly, it's what is best for both of us at this point. And I think it might be the only chance this pub has, too. I'll put the loan in my name, but you know this place is still always going to be yours and Dad's."

"It was always all of ours. This was always for the family." Kyle stood up and walked to the doorway, looking out into the darkened front room. "I had a good run with this place. But I think you'll do better with it."

Ryan gave him a sad smile. "Dad was always proud of your woodworking. Always said you'd make a real success of it someday."

Kyle hadn't ever heard his father say that, and he stared at his brother in wonder. "Really?"

Ryan nodded. "He was proud of you, Kyle. He still is. And to be honest, I always felt like I let him down, never showing much enthusiasm for the pub, not pitching in after he was gone. Now, it might be a chance to redeem that."

"Just don't go changing it too much," Kyle warned, laughing.

"Only for the better," Ryan promised. "There's too much history here to throw away."

Kyle nodded and slowly walked out of the building onto the dark and empty street, possibly for the last time, or at least a long time. There was another part of his history he needed to honor, too. If he could just figure out how to best do that.

*

Brooke hadn't considered how exhausting a busy day in the shop could be. Between the Pine Falls client, two more custom orders, and what was starting to feel like a four-hour meeting with Candy, she couldn't wait to turn the sign on the door and crawl into bed.

Unfortunately, if she did that, she'd never find the time to actually make any of the gowns for the orders that had been placed.

She'd need help, and soon. Designing dresses was where her heart was, not in just selling them.

Candy sat on the small sofa next to her, sipping her tea and staring at the designs Brooke had sketched. "I can't decide," she finally said.

Yes, Brooke had gathered that much, about three cups of tea ago.

"I've waited so long for this day," Candy explained, her big eyes pleading. "I want it to be perfect."

Maybe it wasn't the best sales line, and maybe Brooke was out of patience, but she decided to speak the honest truth. "There's no such thing as perfect, Candy."

Candy frowned a little but didn't protest.

"I once thought I had the perfect wedding," Brooke said plainly, "and then my marriage fell apart. I didn't look back on my wedding day often, didn't stare at any photos, either. I started thinking of it as a day where everything had gone wrong and could have been better. But recently I've realized that wasn't the case. I did have a beautiful wedding. Sometimes emotions can taint our memory in different directions." She sighed and looked at her hands. "I think what I'm saying is that so long as you and Uncle Dennis are happy together, then nothing can ruin your wedding day. It will always be a day that you remember as the happiest, most beautiful day of your life, one that you wouldn't have wanted to change, at all."

Candy wiped a tear from her eye. "You certainly know a lot about love. And here I thought I was the expert."

Brooke shook her head sadly. "I know nothing about love, I'm afraid."

Candy set her tea down and handed over the papers with a huff. "I think you do. More than you realize, or maybe more than you want to admit. So I'm going to trust you, and not just because every design you have shown me has been gorgeous. Which one do you think is best for me?"

"Oh, no. This is your day. Your dress. You have to follow your heart. It will never let you down."

Candy squeezed her hand. "In that case, I need the ballgown. The train. Twenty-five feet."

Brooke laughed. "It's exactly what I would have chosen for you."

Candy stood. "I should let you go. It's late and I've already kept you too long."

"Not at all," Brooke said. "There's always time for family."

Candy beamed. "Family. I like the sound of that."

Brooke's heart still felt heavy as she turned the sign on the door and watched Candy leave. Family. She liked the sound of it too.

Still, there was a part of her past that she hadn't found again when she'd moved back to Blue Harbor, one she hadn't even thought she wanted at the time. One perfect day that she would try to hold onto, not forget.

She walked to the back room, where the wedding dress she'd brought from her parents' attic hung on the door, airing out from years in the trunk. She ran her fingers over the skirt and along the back row of buttons, remembering how her mother had carefully fastened each one and then squeezed her shoulders, staring at their reflection in the mirror.

It had been such a happy day.

Without thinking about it, Brooke slipped out of the dress she was wearing and carefully maneuvered the gown off its hanger, half-surprised to find that it still fit. She walked into the dressing room, her breath catching as she approached the three-way mirror, and she closed her eyes against the image, allowing herself to remember the feel of this gown, the walk down the aisle, the image of Kyle waiting for her, grinning that boyish smile of his. She'd suddenly felt so shy.

But oh, she'd never been more certain.

In the storefront, the door jangled and her eyes sprung open. Candy, probably, back for her sketches, reconsidering the train length, no doubt. Twenty-five feet was...cumbersome. To put it lightly.

The skirt of the gown swished as she turned, and her mouth fell when she saw Kyle standing in the opening to the dressing rooms, staring at her with the same sense of wonder in his eyes he'd had all those years back when she'd first worn it.

"Kyle." She swallowed hard, feeling the need to explain, but not sure what to even say. She owned a wedding dress shop. She could claim this was research. But they both knew that wasn't the case. He knew her too well.

Then. And now.

"The door was unlocked," he said. He shook his head as if clearing his thoughts. "That dress..."

She couldn't believe he remembered it. But then, he remembered everything, didn't he?

Her heart felt heavy when she thought of the dates, the thought he'd put into them, the way she'd kept her guard up. Maybe rightfully so.

"You altered it yourself," he said. "You even thought about making your own, but you weren't sure you'd be able to do it."

"Really?" She'd forgotten the doubt. She'd forgotten a lot.

He nodded. "It's funny how that worked out full circle. Now here you are."

She nodded, trying to swallow back the lump in her throat. "Now here I am. Back in Blue Harbor. Giving other people their perfect day. It's hard not to feel like I've given up a lot, and not just my dreams of making it big in New York."

She gave him a pleading look, one that was part apology, part desperation, because what was done was done, there was no going back now. They'd made their choices, years ago, and here they stood, as two separate people, who used to mean everything to each other.

"Sometimes our dreams take a different shape." He gave her a sad smile. "Besides, you didn't give up on yours; you just altered it a bit. Whereas I..." He pulled in a big breath. "I gave up on my dream a long time ago, managed to forget about it, really, but you...you helped me remember what I once wanted."

She stared at him, a smile creeping at the corners of her mouth. "You're going to start designing furniture again."

He nodded. "But that's not all, Brooke. That's not enough. It was never enough. And it never could be. That dream...it only really mattered because you were a part of it. We imagined that life together."

"Kyle, I—" She didn't need the loan, not really. She could close the shop on more days, use them to sew. She could compromise. She could give up her dream so he could have his.

So they could be together.

But he held up a hand, stopping her. "Please. There's something I need to say. Something you need to know." He shoved his hands into his pockets and looked her in the eye. "I'm not selling the house."

She blinked, unsure of what to say to that. "Okay."

"The bar was all I had left of my father, Brooke. But that house...it was all I had left of you."

Tears stung her eyes as he stepped toward her. "I didn't support your dreams before, you were right."

"No, Kyle," she said sadly. "We didn't support each other. We couldn't. We wanted two different things."

"All I ever wanted was you," he said quietly. "I lost you once, Brooke. I don't want to lose you again."

"What are you saying?" she whispered.

"I'm saying that I love you, Brooke. I never stopped. And I don't think that I ever will. You were my past. My present. And I never stopped wishing or hoping that somehow, you'd be my future."

A tear rolled down her cheek and she brushed it away, even though she was smiling now, straight from the heart. "We lost a lot of time, Kyle."

"What's six years when we could have sixty more?" He grinned. "You never did give me that sixth date. And I have a pretty good idea for it."

"Oh, yeah?"

"Flowers," he said, stepping toward her. "Music. Dancing. Yes, again," he added before she could stop him. "You. Me. All of our nearest and dearest."

She blinked at him, wondering if he was actually saying what she thought he was saying.

"Kyle." The words choked out of her, but she wasn't going to try to stop him.

She stared at him as he dropped to one knee and opened his palm to reveal a small circle of grapevines. It was dried out, brittle even, but it was the first ring he'd given her. The first promise he'd made.

One that he intended to keep.

"Brooke Conway, will you do me the honor of staying my wife?"

She laughed because if she didn't laugh, she would cry. Only it was no use because she was already crying. Only these weren't the tears of hurt and sadness that she had shed in the weeks and months after she'd left for New York. These were the best kind of tears. The happy tears. Because she was happy. Right here, in Blue Harbor, with Kyle Harrison. Forever.

epilogue

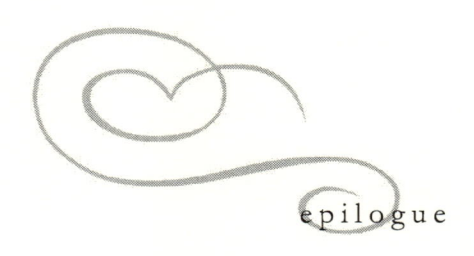

Technically, it was their sixth wedding anniversary, but today it was the first day of the rest of their lives together. Here in Blue Harbor, where they could have everything they had ever wanted.

"I can't believe you're getting married. *Again*." Gabby set her hands on her hips, but there was a shine in her eyes that gave away her happiness.

"It's a vow renewal ceremony," Brooke reminded her sister. It hadn't been easy telling their family that they had never officially ended their marriage, but rather than be upset, everyone had been thrilled at the news.

"Well, whatever you're calling it, I'm happy for you."

"That makes two of us."

Brooke turned to see her mother standing in the doorway of her childhood bedroom. Her eyes were a little more wrinkled at the corners and her hair was a bit greyer at the temple than it had been six years ago, but her smile was still as bright.

"Oh, Brooke. That dress."

Brooke caught her reflection and smiled at what she saw. It was her own dress. Her own creation. A dress to build a dream on.

"Is everyone here?" Brooke didn't dare look out the window for fear of jinxing anything, because even though she said she didn't believe in fate, she did believe in superstition.

And maybe fate, she thought, with a small smile. More than once, she wondered how life might have been if her boss hadn't finally let her go from a job that she should have left years ago, and couldn't bring herself to admit was all wrong for her in every possible way.

"The seats are filling up and the music has started. Listen."

They'd agreed to a backyard ceremony, something simple, with only their closest relatives. There would still be cake, of course, made by Maddie. And wine, Conway brand, no question. Amelia had insisted on catering the event, and Candy had insisted on helping, and now Brooke owed Amelia a drink for that one, but she didn't mind. Amelia was like a sister, and she was looking forward to a chance to catch up more, and to tell her every little detail, this time holding nothing back.

It was one of the many perks to coming back to Blue Harbor. The shop was great, but it was the people who mattered most. And always had.

Brooke inched toward the window, careful to stand in the shadows of the curtain, listening to the sound of Jenna on the piano, filling the lovely spring air with the very piece she had played when she'd once walked down the aisle, as Brooke's bridesmaid.

"I suppose we should go." Brooke set a hand to her stomach.

"Nervous?" Gabby's eyes widened in slight alarm, but Brooke shook her head.

"Excited," she said, squeezing her sister's hand.

They walked down the stairs, Brooke's mother in front, Gabby trailing behind, everyone careful to make sure that no one accidentally stepped on the dress. Once, that would have been a valid concern, but now, nothing could stop this day from being perfect.

"You almost forgot!" Gabby hurried to the dining room and returned with a large bouquet in soft spring colors, shades of ivory and apricot, and hints of green. Brooke couldn't name any of the varieties other than the roses, but she recognized them all the same.

It was her wedding bouquet.

"It's lovely, Gabby Thank you." She felt her eyes mist but Gabby held up a hand.

"There's only one rule. You must toss it in my direction. Give me a fighting chance."

"It's a promise," she said, taking in a breath.

Gabby and her mother left her then, hurrying out the back door and onto the grass, where they made their way up the aisle that divided the two sets of chairs.

"You ready, sweetheart?" Her father turned from the window and looked at her, his eyes tearing just as they had all those years ago.

"More than you can ever know," she said, linking her arm through his.

The sun was warm on her skin as they stepped outside, and the chords from Jenna's piano filled the yard, that had otherwise fallen hush.

Except…

Was that crying that she heard?

Her eyes scanned the crowd as her father led her to the aisle and fell upon Candy, in head to toe pink, sobbing loudly into a lace handkerchief, but grinning ear to ear.

Brooke caught her cousin Amelia fighting off a grin and rolling her eyes skyward as she turned to stand at the end of the aisle, but by then, she was already smiling. Not at the sounds of Candy loudly blowing her nose as the music swelled, but at the sight of her husband, standing a few yards in front of her.

Waiting for her.

ABOUT THE AUTHOR

Olivia Miles is a *USA Today* bestselling author of feel-good women's fiction with a romantic twist. She has frequently been ranked as an Amazon Top 100 author, and her books have appeared on several bestseller lists, including Amazon charts, BookScan, and USA Today. Treasured by readers across the globe, Olivia's heart-warming stories have been translated into German, French, and Hungarian, with editions in Australia in the United Kingdom.

Olivia lives on the shore of Lake Michigan with her family.

Visit www.OliviaMilesBooks.com for more.

Made in the USA
Las Vegas, NV
26 April 2021